bookmark for the heart

Small Town Talk

Book One

charlotte northeast

Cover Art by Fers

@thefangomaster

Printed in the USA

First edition, 2025.

ISBN - 978-1-968357-09-2

Dedicated to book nerds (and lovers) everywhere…

also from trashcan publishing

- **SABINE AND THE SILVER HAMMER** by Charlotte Northeast - Assisted Sinning, Book 1
- **CARTEL BOMBSHELL** by Didi Pounder
- **RED HOT BLACKTOP** by Didi Pounder
- **DOWN FOR THE COUNT** by Ailis Elliot

one

. . .

Emily

"They have a margarita *station*, Em," Brittany gushes into the phone. "I swear, an entire bar where you can have anything you want. We could get so messed up!"

She always talks like this, but today it's too early and *way* too over the top for me. Since she can't see me, I don't think twice about rolling my eyes.

"Wow, Britt. It sounds tempting, believe me—" Before I can get out another word, Britt charges over the top of me. She's far too hyped up to do something as simple as *listen*.

"Just get out here, Em. Cider Mill Valley has nothing to offer. It's a dead town. Think of all the cute things you could make here. All the cool artists you would meet. You need to move in with me, like, last week…"

I pull the phone away from my ear, not eager to have this same, tired conversation again. She's got a point about meeting artists and broadening my horizons, but all I can think is how I'd get lost in an actual city.

Not physically, per se—I just can't shake the notion I'd

lose *myself*. And given that I've just put the pieces back together after my breakup, I'm not itching to throw them to the wind again.

Should I leave this small town? Probably. I've been here my whole life, after all — but something just won't let me go. Call it nerves, or being shy… I do everything I can to not put a label to it. Whatever it is, it's mighty powerful.

"Wow," a little girl cries, and I look down the counter to catch sight of my coworker Mark. He's performing a magic trick for a kid on the other side of the register, and I smile in spite of myself. He's always pulling stuff like this. Britt chatters away in my ear, but I'm barely paying attention.

I shouldn't have even answered my phone in the first place.

If my boss Annette saw me, I'd get the side eye for sure. Maybe even a little more. But for now, I'm safe. Annette's a night owl so we won't see her until sometime after lunch. For the most part, Mark and I run the bookstore pretty much on our own, which suits me fine.

Besides, there isn't much going on. On weekdays when school is in session, this place can be a ghost town.

A ghost-town-bookstore inside of a ghost-town-town, I muse. It's an entertaining thought, but it doesn't do anything to help me to focus on my job. Instead, I concentrate on Mark's little performance.

Leaning against the doorway that leads into the back room, I watch the little girl's eyes widen as he throws a quarter into the air and then seemingly catches it behind her ear.

The kid's high-pitched laugh fills the store, her fat, ginger ringlets bouncing right along with her giggles. Her grandmother laughs with her, clearly happy she doesn't have to be her granddaughter's sole source of entertainment for the moment.

Once the impromptu show is over, Mark puts their books

in a bag, hands the grandmother her receipt, and they leave the store with big, silly grins.

Another satisfied customer.

Or *customers*, I guess.

Funny thing is, I find I'm grinning too.

"Emily," Britt asks, jolting me out of my reverie. "Are you there?"

"Sorry, Britt," I reply, my cheeks flushing in embarrassment at having tuned her out. "I gotta call you back. I'm at work. You know how it is." But does she? Britt's out there drinking at margarita stations and doing whatever else people do in the big city. I'm not sure she has the first idea about *how it is.*

Britt sighs over the line, clearly put out.

"Sure. Fine. Whatever. But get here, Em. *Soon.* I mean, the margarita bar alone is—" I click the line dead.

Exhaling in frustration, I put the phone down and look over my shoulder to find Mark smiling at me, a twinkle in his deep blue eyes. He's never met Britt, but he's around me enough to know the deal by now. And he's never above razzing me about it.

Which I'm weirdly okay with. I've only known him a few months, but he already has a place in my life that feels like we've been friends forever. Like we've always known each other but didn't cross paths until the right time. He's always there when I need him. Always ready with a smile or a joke.

Or a glance. Don't forget those.

Maybe I'm wrong, but sometimes when he looks at me, I can almost swear he's checking me out. It makes me blush every single time—almost as much as I'm sure he'd blush if he knew I did the same every now and then. It's nothing serious, but it's sneaky fun all the same.

Facing him now, I swear I almost caught one of his extra-attentive glances. He looks away quickly and as usual, his chestnut hair flops over his forehead, giving him the look of someone always caught in a windstorm.

It suits him. The guy positively radiates warmth. I can't put my finger on it exactly, but there's an ease about him that calms me down no matter what's going on in my day. I've worked retail most of my life, and a little bookshop like TurnLeaf Corner has its perks, but people can be people no matter where you are.

Thankfully, Mark always manages to make the shifts feel shorter. And more fun.

"You've done it again," I say, walking towards the counter. "Charmed that little girl something fierce."

Mark leans towards me, his plaid shirt pulling tight across his shoulders.

"Let's see the big online retailers do *that*. We little guys will always find a way to survive," he chuckles, shutting the cash register with a flourish.

I laugh, sliding behind the counter next to him so I can pretend to work.

The store is empty. Outside, the midday lunch crowd is just starting to leave their offices and amble towards the diner across the street. Bored office workers happy for a reprieve from their desk jobs. All the little shops and buildings that make up the business sector—such as it is—in Cider Mill Valley.

Gauzy sunlight splashes on the pavement so that Main Street almost glows. It rained last night so everything looks a little shiny. A little fresh.

Britt can say whatever she wants, it's little things like this that make it hard to leave. Little magical moments I'd miss out on in the city. I'm sure it's got plenty of its own, but at times like this, I think my simple life is pretty hard to beat.

"So, uh…" Mark taps his pen on a stack of new fiction that just arrived. "These aren't going to shelve themselves." Giving Mark a snort, I grab up the pile.

"I didn't realize your legs were broken?"

"Hey, somebody's got to watch the register. What if somebody tried to rob the place?"

"Your lips to—" I start to reply, but I stop dead in my tracks.

Something outside has shifted, and my body reacts before my eyes can focus. The warm, cozy room goes icy cold. I shiver, almost dropping the pile of books. My mouth dries out, my breathing goes shallow.

Oh, my God.

It's Leon.

My dark cloud of an ex-boyfriend.

two

. . .

"**E**mily? You okay?"

In the space of half a second she's gone deathly pale and started shaking like a leaf.

"Earth to Em." I try to sound casual, but my voice betrays me by cracking just a little.

Whenever I see her upset my heart actually hurts. Whether it's because a customer was rude, or because her best friend won't stop pestering her to leave town, my chest aches for her.

"Uh." She licks her lips. I can tell just from her voice that her mouth has dried out. "It's just that Leon is across the street." An unaccountable shudder steals over me, but I try to ignore it.

"Who's Leon?" Maybe he's somebody who used to bully her at school. Or a jerk from her old job. He could be anybody, but when she turns those shimmering eyes on me, there's no question.

"My ex-boyfriend."

I'm next to her in a flash, pushing up my glasses to squint out the window to see if I can spot him. Surely he'll be hard to pick out of the lunch rush—right?

Wrong.

Just from looking at the guy I can tell I don't like him. Even from this distance, he's clearly out of place. Cider Mill Valley just doesn't seem to suit him. And he damn sure doesn't suit Cider Mill Valley.

Brown-black hair, styled slick and rigid, leather jacket, and dark denim jeans completing the look. He's like something out of a movie. Topped off with a set of smoldering eyes that swallow up all the sunshine on the block.

Leon, huh?

This is the first I've heard of him. I have to admit I did some stealthy scouting after I met Emily a few months ago. I've only managed to learn a handful of things about her.

One, she's single.

Two, unlike me, she's lived in Cider Mill Valley all her life.

And three? Well, three was obvious. I like her a lot. Like, a *whole* lot.

Not that she seems to notice.

"I had no idea he was back in town…" she mutters faintly before her words drift off.

I take the stack of books from her and set them on the counter.

"Okay. So, he's here," I shrug. "So what?"

"It's just…" The wildest thing happens. She starts to *laugh.* "It's like seeing a dinosaur in your backyard. Or a car in your living room. Totally improbable." It's such a relief to see her laughing, I join in. Maybe she was just startled. Maybe it's not as big a deal as I thought.

But then her laughter cuts short.

"Shit," she whispers.

"What?" I ask, even though I don't have to.

"Mark, I think he's heading this way."

I'm at her side again like lightning. Sure as anything, the shady customer is on the curb, looking lazily from side to side. To hell with the fact there's a crosswalk fifteen feet away. Evidently, those things are for suckers.

"Uh, huh." Thinking he might actually set foot in here, Emily's terror rubs off on me. My heart rate spikes, and I try to stay calm. "Look, so what if he does? I mean, what's the big deal?"

"I just..." Those gimlet eyes flash at me. "If he comes in here, he can't know I'm single. Leon is a lot of not great things, but if he thinks I'm with someone, he'll leave me alone. I'm sure of it."

I look back out at the dark figure ambling across the street. He's got a swagger, alright. The walk of a man used to getting what he wants. The guy seems to be built entirely of hard edges. It's hard to imagine a sweet girl like Emily being with a guy like him.

"Listen," I say, trying to be helpful. "I know it's none of my business, Em. Just know you don't owe that guy anything. And if you need him to go away, we can make that happen." I step closer to her, not really sure I can make good on a promise like that. Or what it might actually mean.

Taking on the likes of someone like Leon is a tall order. But for Emily's sake, I'm willing to do anything.

She nods as she takes this in, then her eyes flash, boring into me. There's something slightly crazed—almost feral—behind them. She's got an idea, and I get the sinking feeling I'm not going to like it.

"Mark." She grabs my hand, a desperate smile painting her lips. "Can you pretend to be my boyfriend?" My first reaction is to pull away, but she grips even tighter. "I know it sounds crazy, but trust me. No strings attached. You don't have to do anything. Just sell it so that he thinks we're a couple. Like, in love."

Did I say I'd do anything for her? Maybe not everything...

"Em... I... uh..."

My ears start to ring, and I tell myself I didn't hear what I just thought I did. I mean, did she really just ask me to pretend I'm in love with her?

What a performance that would be.

The pain in my heart triples in the space of a second. No longer an ache, it's now a full-on stabbing sensation. I reach up to put a hand on my chest, half expecting to find blood there.

No blood. But the pain is real. As is Emily's request.

Even more agonizing, those crystal eyes—the ones I can't get out of my head—stare into my face. Open. Hopeful.

Waiting for an answer.

"Emily..." Her name sticks on my lips. "I get that you're anxious, but I don't think I can do that."

Her face falls, but before we can chase this wild scenario any further, the bell above the door jingles and Leon darkens the doorway.

"You guys are open, right?" Is it just me, or is the guy just a *little* too loud for an empty store?

I can't speak.

I mean, did Emily really just ask me to pretend to be her boyfriend to get her out of an awkward conversation?

It's hard enough having a massive crush on your co-worker, it's another thing to be her personal prop.

But at least I told her. At least I said no.

Even if it hurts.

Swallowing hard, I open my mouth to reply but Emily beats me to it.

"Uhh. Yeah. We're open. Hi, Leon. Didn't you know you were in town," Emily says, her voice just as loud as Leon's but way less confident.

The guy shoots her a lopsided grin and immediately I know why women are attracted to this guy. He's got that thing women love to hate: he's giving off that *I can be the one to fix him* vibe.

"Yeah. For a work thing." Leon hooks his thumb through his belt and cocks his hip. "Setting up the new banking systems. Just a few weeks. Heard you were working here. Wanted to see if the rumors were true."

There's that rakish smile again. And there's more than a hint of brag when he talks about his job. At the same time, his voice is low, wet gravel on a sunny beach. Yet another reason to dislike this guy on sight.

Emily laughs. Another emotion joins the pile.

Betrayal.

I have never heard her laugh like that before, and I thought I'd cornered the market on making that girl laugh. At least I can comfort myself that the sound coming out of her isn't real. It's like the *idea* of a laugh. Like a crude approximation. This isn't the Emily I know.

"You heard right," she says, leaning against a display. "I've been here a little while now." Even her stance is awkward. All the same, Leon looks her up and down without even trying to hide his overt appraisal. He clicks his teeth at the sight of her. Another trait that puts me on edge.

"You doing good?" he asks, his tongue playing over his teeth. Annoyingly, those, too, are perfect. A row of gleaming soldiers nestled in his mouth.

Another giggle escapes Emily. Or something like a giggle.

"Uhh… yup. Doing great," she says. Her fingers flit over to the nearest table as if trying to find a handhold. Something to grip onto. They land on the stack of books she brought over just moments ago, fumbling one to the floor. It slaps to the wood surface with a loud clap, and I jump about three feet while Emily lets out a little shriek. An obvious overreaction on both our parts, and there's no question Leon clocks it.

Lying there splayed open on the worn wooden floor, the book looks sad. Forlorn.

For some reason, I'm jealous of the damn thing. Being sad seems like a freaking vacation compared to the crazy number of feelings ping ponging inside me right now.

"Whoopsie." Leon clicks his teeth again and makes no move to help Emily retrieve the book. "Butterfingers." There's something nefarious in the way he says it that makes me bristle. Like an insult masquerading as a term of affection.

My hatred of the man grows more every second. He's been in here—what? Two minutes? And already I could throttle him. A new record for me. I like to think I'm a pretty affable guy.

"Oh, gosh! Oh! I… uh…" Emily stammers. Seemingly incapable of picking up the book.

I head towards her, but something stops me. There's an aura around that guy that feels almost like a forcefield. Like I don't want to go near it. Or him, rather.

Collar-Up Leon is completely unperturbed but turns his attention to me like he's clocking me for the very first time.

"Sup?" he says, cocking his stubbled chin in my general direction.

"Hey," I croak, bending down to grab the book. When I stand back up, Emily is right next to me, her whole body thrumming with nerves. With a slight tremor in her hand, she touches my upper arm. A heady mix of elation and dread courses through me.

There's no way she's going to do this.

"Hey, so… this is Mark. He works here too. And…" Her eyes flick to me, but they're glassy with forced confidence. "He's my boyfriend."

Did she really just say that? Even after I asked her not to?

Now it's Leon's turn to be shocked. The dark curtain of his eyebrows raises up into his jagged hairline. The corner of his mouth curls slightly and his eyes turn to me again, this time scrutinizing me in a whole new light.

"Really?" How is it possible to cram that much derision into a single word? My whole body gets numb and tingly.

A tense silence fills the store as the three of us stare at each other. I can't begin to read what's going on in Emily's head.

Emily may be my crush, but she isn't perfect. If I'm being honest, she's always using me in some way. Most of the time, it's harmless. I'm Mr. Reliable. Mr. Good Time. I know it's something she does, and usually, I can justify it.

Hell, sometimes I even crave it.

Not today. Not for this.

three

<u>Emily</u>

Finally, I find a scrap of courage. Or something close to it, anyway.

"Are you looking for something in particular?" I ask, my pitch sky-high. I can always count on my voice to betray me.

Leon looks at me, his sculpted dark eyebrows creasing together in confusion.

"Uhhh. No." God, his voice practically drips with condescension. "This isn't exactly my scene. I just wanted to say hi."

His eyes snag on the small display full of stationary and funky pens near the door. It's proudly topped with my greeting cards. The ones I make in my spare time. The ones my boss has so graciously agreed to sell. Not that they sell much.

I cringe as a flicker of recognition glints in his eyes. If only the floor would open up and swallow me.

"Huh." He walks over, picking one up and turning it in his hands. "Still doing that doodling thing, huh? Wow."

Somehow the 'wow' isn't exactly a compliment. I shrug, dying inside. There's that familiar feeling of everything I do being inadequate. Silly in his eyes. I hoped I'd never have to feel that again.

"Anyway." He jams the card back in the rack, a little too ungently for my taste. "I'll be around a few more weeks if you —nah, never mind." Leon cuts himself off, his eyes connecting with Mark again. The poor guy is getting redder by the second.

Shame clouds over me to think that I'm the one who did this to him.

Before I can beat myself up too much, Leon sweeps back to look at me, weighing something in his mind. I know what he's doing. Our relationship may not have been long, but it was long enough for me to see straight through him. He's doing the math. Calculating the amount of risk.

Leon sticks his neck out for nobody. Not even when the prize is high.

"Well, I guess I'll see ya around," he says finally. In a flash, he turns on his boot heel and leaves the store, the doorbell jangling its happy note like a funeral bell.

The whole encounter lasted less than two minutes.

It felt like an eternity.

I release the breath I've been holding. My body goes slack and instantly my muscles feel like bags of cement. Like I need to sleep for three days.

On the bright side, my gamble paid off in one way—it got Leon off my back. But it's not without a cost. With a shrinking feeling, I turn to face Mark. He looks at me with daggers in his eyes.

"Why… Emily, why did you do that?" His voice is hoarse and shaky. "I told you not to."

Swallowing hard, I try to minimize the damage. I never wanted to hurt my friend and yet here I am doing precisely that. Words tumble out of me, my hands flying to my face.

"Mark. I am so, *so* sorry. I just… I panicked. Leon is a really tricky customer, and I just needed to get rid of him fast. And I didn't mean to—"

Mark sighs deeply and cuts me off.

"What does it mean then?" he asks. "Was that it? What happens now?"

No matter how much I try to read his expression, I can't.

Does he want to buy into the lie? Or is he hoping it'll go away?

Scenarios and wild ideas trip through my brain. What am I going to do? How long did Leon say he was going to be in town? A few weeks? What does that mean?

"Ummm." I cringe, knowing how deeply I've screwed up. "Mark, I think we may have to keep the charade going. At least until Leon leaves town. Knowing him, he won't let it go easily. We might have to…" I can't finish the sentence. I have no idea what any of this means.

What the hell have I done? This is bad.

Mark runs his hand through his hair, then takes off his glasses to wipe them on his flannel. The reddish tinge in his cheeks is starting to fade, and I catch myself thinking he's a little bit handsome. Maybe it's because my heart is racing and my brain is cloudy, but it hits me in a way that puts me off center.

Like, I always knew on a surface level that he was good looking, but I'd never really considered it before. A strong jaw but kind eyes. Completely unlike the ex-boyfriend that just left.

"Okay," he says vaguely, putting his glasses back on. When he looks at me again, my friend is nowhere to be found. His expression is all business. "So, what's this going to look like? What do we do?"

"I'm not entirely sure. Maybe just walk around town a little bit together. Maybe go to the movies? Or dinner? You know, the usual stuff," I say, trying to infuse something light into the conversation. *Anything* to get us out of the muddy tension surrounding us.

"Oh, yeah. The usual." Mark scoffs. "And if Leon sees us? Or anyone that knows you sees us? What then? How much PDA are we talking about here?"

Again, his expression is unreadable. Which is wholly unlike him.

Don't forget those stolen glances, Em. They were real. You can't deny it any longer.

"Maybe just a bit," I offer. "Like, hold my hand if we see him? Or I'll kiss you on the cheek? Simple stuff. Like friends… but more…"

I trail off again. I have no idea. This is all uncharted territory.

Territory that I built.

Oh, Em. You've done it again…

Mark sighs again and heads back to the cash register. The muscles in his back strain against his plaid shirt. Is it possible he's ripped under there? How have I never noticed his physique? Was he always that jacked?

As soon as he reaches the counter, he turns around again.

"But what about people who already know us?" It's a fair question, but it hits me in the chest.

I shrug, trying to summon an apathy over the nerves that rattle my entire body.

"We let them in on the ruse. The ones that know Leon will understand."

The phone rings and Mark moves to answer it. Before he does, he asks me one more question.

"And after Leon leaves? What happens then?"

I shake my head, unable to think that far ahead. I can't fake apathy anymore. The enormity of what I've done rushes over me like a tidal wave.

"Let's cross that bridge later, okay?" Even as I say it, I can feel how mousy it sounds. Mark gives an almost imperceptible nod that I can only interpret as consent and answers the phone.

God, I hate this. Hurting Mark is cruel. Like, kicking a puppy level nasty. Why would I want to do that to him?

Then I think about the chaos and drama that would follow Leon breaking back into my life and almost get nauseous.

I did so much soul-searching, cleaning myself up after our tumultuous year-long relationship. He surged into my life like a whirlwind and vanished just as quickly, leaving nothing but destruction behind.

Leon had made me into someone I wasn't proud of. I refused to see his red flags, no matter how hard he waved them. I changed things about myself just to please him. Spent agonizing nights next to my phone hoping he'd call or text. Even went so far as to minimize who I was around him.

I hid my art supplies and completely stopped talking about what I wanted to do with my card making business. Because I knew he thought it was frivolous. Stupid, even. It amazed me how he could hurt me with whatever he had to say. Or didn't say.

Or did.

Or didn't do.

Whenever I thought I'd figured him out, just when I thought I'd found the even ground in our relationship, he would cause a seismic shift. His leaving for Chicago was the greatest thing to happen to me. Although it didn't feel that way at the time.

Turns out it was distance that I needed to rid myself of him. To heal myself. And the greatest thing of all, to like myself again.

That was no small feat.

And now, here he is, back in Cider Mill Valley.

Months of work could be unraveled in mere seconds.

Much as I'd like it to, none of that justifies what I just did to Mark. A sour feeling in the pit of my stomach tells me I've really screwed him over on this one. Especially since he specifically said he wouldn't do it. And I threw him under the bus.

Squaring my shoulders, I try to make light of it. Pretend it's not a big deal.

It's just a lark. It'll all pass. In time, I think frantically, trying to keep from hyperventilating.

And if it doesn't? Well, I can always move to the big city. Britt will be thrilled.

four

. . . . .

Mark

I haven't slept in two days. For obvious reasons. Strangely enough, things at the bookshop haven't changed a bit. At least not so long as the place is empty. I was worried Emily and I would be weird around each other after this little Faustian bargain we've made, but thank God we've been perfectly comfortable.

Every time that bell jingles, however—it's showtime. Emily finds me wherever I am and sneaks her arm through mine, or puts her hand on me somehow.

It may be all for show, but I get all tingly every time. Some folks clock it and some folks don't, but it doesn't matter to me. All these little gifts of affection thrown my way are welcome. Even if they slip away the second the door closes again.

That said, Leon hasn't so much as looked through our window since he first showed up. A big part of me is relieved I don't have to navigate that posing jackass again, but I can't

19

help wondering just who we're doing all this for. My impression was that this whole thing was to keep Emily safe from him, but what's the point if he's not around?

So, Emily has decided on the nuclear option.

We're going on an actual date.

Well, maybe not an *actual* date, but we're going into public with the intention of being seen as a couple. Regardless of whether Leon is anywhere to see us.

Emily wants to get the word out, and I get to spend time with her outside the bookshop, so I'll take it.

Real or not, I can't help getting excited for the date.

I know I shouldn't. It was implicit that feelings aren't part of the deal here. Trouble is, I can't help it. My feelings are there whether I want them or not, and I catch myself wondering if the same is true for Emily.

My nerves are so high I walk around Emily's block three times before ringing the bell for her apartment. I left the house early out of sheer anxiety, so it's mainly to keep from showing up fifteen minutes early.

If I had hoped walking around the block would settle my jitters, I was wrong. If anything, I'm worried I'll sweat through my shirt before she sees me. Which would be a real shame, because I took all day picking my outfit. We want people to buy into this, sure, but deep down I want to look my best for *her*.

"Woah," she gasps when the door to her building opens and Emily steps out. "You look great!" Her face shines in a way that makes my chest throb.

"Thanks." I duck my chin just a bit to hide how pleased I am she said that. "So do you."

Truer words have never been spoken. Emily is always beautiful in the shop, but tonight she's downright ravishing.

All those waves of red hair are swept back into a ponytail tied with a green ribbon. It spills down over her skin in an off the shoulder sweater. I don't know if I've ever seen her shoulders before, and they're peppered with freckles that make my knees weak.

A little pendant hangs on her chest, and I have to work to keep from staring at it. The darn thing is like an invitation to look at her breasts, and much as I'd like to give in, Emily deserves better than to be ogled.

"Look at us," Emily says softly after we appraise each other for a second. "Almost like the real thing."

Almost.

That one word sours in the pit of my stomach.

Despite that, I offer her my arm and lead her down the sidewalk toward the restaurant. We've decided to skip the diner in hopes of making more of a splash. The idea is if anybody asks, we say it's our anniversary.

But as we make our way down the street, nobody looks at us twice. I'm not sure what we expected, but it's not like we're making any kind of waves.

Not that I'm complaining.

Emily has put on some perfume for the occasion, and the floral scent mixes with her usual aroma of vanilla until my head is spinning. Everything about this woman is irresistible.

I hold the door for her when we reach Nona Bella. It's a simple gesture, but I can't help wondering if Leon ever had the presence of mind to do it for her. Something tells me more often than not he left Emily to fend for herself. That's if he ever took her to a place as nice as this.

By small town standards, Nona Bella is really something. Linen tablecloths and real candles. Most of the other places in Cider Mill Valley are perfectly happy with battery operated tea lights.

Determined to one-up Leon in any way I can, I make a point of pulling out Emily's chair.

"Oh!" Surprised her, alright. She rewards me with the brightest smile imaginable. "Thank you."

"Of course, my dear." Whoops! Those last two words just

slipped out. We haven't discussed pet names or terms of affection, but I couldn't help myself. What burns most is how natural it felt saying that to her. As I seat myself, I search her face to see if I've overstepped. Far from it, it seems.

She's taking things in with a funny grin that's almost melancholy.

"I've lived here my whole life and almost never come in here," she muses.

"Is that right? When was the last time?" The question catches her, and she looks at me with the candlelight dancing in her green eyes.

"We came for my mom's birthday when I was… eleven, I think? Maybe twelve? Anyway, she leans closer and drops her voice. "Nothing's changed." A wicked glint in her eye invites a chuckle I have to suppress.

"Oh, yeah?"

"Like…" She steals a sneaky look around before meeting my eyes again. "I'm not even sure they've *dusted*."

I have hide my mouth behind my napkin to keep from guffawing.

"Well, I think it's *nice*," I say when I get myself together. "Let's just hope they pay more attention to keeping the kitchen clean." That gets a snicker out of Emily, and I get the very real feeling we're going to be the biggest troublemakers this place has seen in a while. We haven't even ordered yet, and already I can tell we're going to spend the whole evening cracking each other up.

By the time our meal arrives, we're in suppressed hysterics. I'd say it's because we're hilarious, but the bottle of very good wine is probably helping.

"Oh, my goodness," Emily coos as our waiter sets a plate in front of her. "This looks *exquisite*." If only she could see it from where I'm sitting. The plate of grilled shrimp looks delectable, but it can't hope to compare with the woman I'm seated across from. Her pale skin glows in the candlelight, each flicker accentuating her long neck and sparkling eyes. It's been a battle not to spend the whole evening gazing at her in pure wonder.

Then she cuts a bite and has a taste. The way the fork slips past her lips leaves me helplessly wishing I knew what they felt like. Her eyes flutter closed, and she lifts her chin with a groan, savoring the bite. It's an act of innocent enjoyment, but there's something so sensual in it I almost melt in my seat.

When her eyes drift open again, she beams with satisfaction.

"How's yours," she asks.

"Perfect." That gets a laugh, and she looks at me sideways.

"You haven't even picked up your fork yet." She's right, and I get all flustered at being caught out. "Anyway…" She dismisses the moment with a wave. "Before you do, here." She cuts another bite of shrimp and extends her fork to me. "You *have* to try this."

The forkful hovers in front of me, and my heart starts to pound.

Is she really going to feed me with her own fork?

The fork that just touched her lips?

I lean forward and have a taste. Not of the shrimp. Who cares about that? Every fiber of me is searching the tines for traces of her. Relishing the proxy of a kiss.

"Divine," I say as she settles back in her chair.

"It's really great, right?"

"Better than I could have imagined."

This is even more dangerous than I was afraid it would be. Because it's so easy to trick myself into thinking it's all real. Which, of course, it isn't.

I should probably just enjoy it while I can. Stack up the little moments of joy as keepsakes of this stolen time.

Instead, a strange melancholy creeps in to ruin it all. Looking at her like this—being with her like this—is almost painful in its beauty.

Perfect as all this is, I'm not sure how long I can keep this up.

five

. . .

Emily.

Why is it that every time I catch sight of Leon, I'm on my own? Granted, it's not like I expect him to come back into the book shop. If anything, that's the one place I should be safe from him. Which is fine with me because it's more or less my safe space anyway. My refuge.

There are plenty of reasons for that, but I don't want to think about them too hard.

Let's be real. Mark is a big part of that.

I liked working with Annette before, but it wasn't really anything more than a job. But since Mark joined the party, TurnLeaf Corner has become one of my favorite places on the planet. It's something else to actually look forward to going to work every day.

When I'm not there? It's like Leon is around every corner. That's the main reason why Mark and I had to take our little show on the road.

Again, I didn't think Leon would be at Nona Bella, but surely we would have run into him on the street before or after, right? I'd almost be disappointed we didn't if Mark hadn't made everything so easy.

A day later I spot Leon in the grocery store while I'm grabbing a few things for the weekend. By the beer cooler, of course.

"Shit," I whisper to myself, crouching down behind the bell peppers. I don't think he spotted me, which means I have two options.

One, I can go about my business and ignore the guy.

Two, I can hightail it out of here and avoid confrontation altogether.

Much as I hate to be a coward, I find myself leaning towards the second. Looking down at my arm basket, I take stock of just what I actually need right now.

There's nothing I can't come back for tomorrow.

A dozen eggs stare back up at me along with a carton of creamer. Breakfast is bound to be pretty sad without them, but I'll just have to manage.

Staying low, I scurry as fast as I can for the doors, my heart in my throat. A group of ladies lined up at the register look at me like a five headed cockroach, but I can't work myself up enough to care. Weird looks are a lot less harrowing than bumping into my ex. Without Mark here to hide behind, I feel completely naked. And I promised myself when I finally got my life together again that I'd never be naked around Leon again.

Out on the street I can breathe a little easier, but only a little.

My apartment is just a couple blocks away, so I break into a sprint. By the time I reach the door to my building, I've got a stitch in my side from running. That doesn't stop me from charging up the stairs. It's not until the door locks behind me that I feel like myself again.

"What am I doing?" I mutter to myself, gasping for air. "What an idiot."

Leon really did a number on me. I thought I was better, but one look at him and it seems like all I do is make stupid decisions.

And drag innocent people into the vortex with me.

Guilt stabs me in the ribs to think of how callously I took advantage of Mark. He was clear as crystal about not wanting any part of this, but I went and did it anyway. When the dust settles from our little charade, I'm going to have to think of something really good to make it up to him.

Everything is just such a mess. The worst part is I haven't really got anybody to talk to about it. If he weren't part of the whole scheme, I'd probably confide in Mark. He's the closest thing I've got to a friend these days, and I've done my best to complicate the hell out of that.

Which leaves only one person.

"Oh, my God, *hiiiii!*" Brittany squeals as soon as she picks up the phone. "I was starting to wonder if you were dead. It's been *forever*."

"Yeah." How is it I already regret deciding to call her? "Things have been pretty crazy around here."

"In Cider Mill Valley? Somehow, I doubt that."

"You have no idea," I say, sighing heavily. Suddenly I'm not sure if I want to confess my situation to Brittany. She's not the most sympathetic ear in the world, but right now she's the only port in this particular storm. I grit my teeth and spill the beans. "Leon's in town."

Brittany gasps so hard I'm surprised she doesn't drop the phone.

"*No!* Wait… you mean, like, *Leon* Leon?"

"I'm afraid so." It stings to lay this out. Britt had a front row seat to our breakup and was practically made out of I-told-you-sos over the whole thing. And here I am ripping the scab off all over again.

"Unreal," Brittany whispers. "Though, actually…" Her

tone alone makes me squirm. "I mean, are you actually surprised?"

"What do you mean?"

"Em!" She laughs. "You're both *from* there, aren't you? It's not like he was going to head off to Chicago never to return. Everybody comes back home eventually."

I've never thought about it before. Which makes me feel even stupider than I already have.

"I suppose…" I mumble, more than a little sheepish.

"Anyway, if I were you, I'd consider this a wake-up call. Like, this is the sign you've been waiting for. If Leon can show up in that tiny town—where there's nowhere to hide from him—and turn your whole life upside down, then what's the point?"

"Yeah." I look around at my little apartment. It's the only place I can actually feel any kind of security. Beyond the bookstore, that is.

My world has gotten pretty small.

"It's like I've been saying over and over, time to ditch that place and come to the city. Get out of there and never look back."

Here we go again. Broken-record-Brittany is off to the races. At the same time, I get the queasy feeling this time she's right. Maybe it really is time to cut ties and get out of here.

Not that I have that many ties to cut.

Well, maybe one…

"I guess I can think about it."

"Don't think," she insists. "Just pack and go. Thinking about it is what's kept you stuck there for so long. I mean, how are you even surviving with Leon hanging around town? You must be so lonely."

The funny thing is, I don't. Apart from right now, obviously. But most of the time, lonely is the furthest thing from what I feel. If I'm being honest, that pretty much all comes down to Mark.

Wait, should I tell Brittany about what we've been doing?

Absolutely not. All she would do is laugh at me. Call me desperate.

But it doesn't feel like desperation. Maybe it did at first, but after several days of play-acting like Mark and I are a couple, desperation is the last thing I feel about it. If anything, our first 'date' was a downright treat. Why would I go and spoil that by telling Brittany?

"I'm getting by," I say vaguely.

"Not much of a life." God, I can hear her smirk over the phone. It makes my temper flare a bit.

"Can't imagine doing much more than that in the city. It's so expensive, and I wouldn't even have a job."

"It's different here. Just 'getting by' is a lot more exciting when there's actually stuff to *do* besides throw rocks in the river or whatever you do to keep busy out there." Now I know for a fact I'm not telling her about Mark. A girl like Brittany would never understand it.

Besides, I've already done enough to hurt him, so why open him up to ridicule from someone who doesn't even know him? Bad enough Britt likes to laugh at me, but Mark deserves better than that. She could never really appreciate a guy like him. If anything, he's too good for her.

"Listen, I should go." I startle myself by saying it without thinking. Clearly it catches Brittany up short as well.

"Oh. Okay…" It almost sounds like I've hurt her feelings. The people pleaser in me rushes to apologize.

"Sorry to dump and dash, but I've got… things to take care of before tomorrow." It's the lamest lie on the planet, and I can tell in an instant I haven't fooled her.

"Fine," she says curtly. "I get it. Hiding from Leon is a full-time job." It's a biting comment, but part of me feels like I deserve it.

"Look, I'll call you soon, alright?"

"Whatever," she grunts. "Just think about what I said.

You'd really have a better time out here. So good that even if you ran into your ex, it wouldn't be enough to get you down." That's a tall promise, and I can't bring myself to imagine it's true.

"Thanks for the offer. I'll… I'll let you know soon."

I end the call feeling even worse than before I dialed her number. Which isn't what friends are supposed to do.

I didn't need her to hector me about moving, I needed comfort. I needed a sympathetic ear.

I needed Mark.

He's the only one who could really calm me down right now.

Looking at the phone in my hands, I contemplate how easy it would be to reach out to him. Even going so far as to scroll down to his contact.

Then I freeze.

I've never actually just *called* him before. We text a little bit, mostly things related to the ruse. To ring him up just to talk feels like it would almost be a transgression. Like, I'm not sure what he does after we part ways, and the last thing I want to do is disturb him at home. Especially just to complain about Leon.

And Brittany. He's heard me moan about her plenty.

All the same, even a quick message would go miles to making me feel better. I just know it.

Opening up the text thread, I type out a quick note.

> Hey! I was thinking maybe we could go out on another mock-date tomorrow night to keep things rolling. What do you say?

Something strikes me wrong. Looking over the message again, I settle on the word *mock*. It just feels icky. But do I really want to just call it a *date*? Wouldn't that muddy the waters?

How could it? We both knew up front what this was going

to be. Surely there's no harm in skipping the 'mock' part? After all, that's more or less implied, right? We both know any date we go on is just part of the plan.

I delete the word.

No sense in rubbing things in any more. He's taking part in this against his will. I don't want him to read it wrong and think that I'm actually mocking him.

I hit send, and the three dot bubble indicating his reply comes up immediately.

Yes.

I slump back on my couch with a relieved sigh. That was so easy.

Why can't everything be this easy?

six

. . .

<u>*Mark*</u>

"That went okay, I think," Emily muses, as we head down the alleyway separating the local movie house from the diner. The tell-tale grit of the diner's signature French fries lingers on my fingertips, something I've come to love about living in Cider Mill Valley.

"Sure," I reply. "Because Shirley doesn't know her head from a hole in the ground." Snarky as I want to be, I can't keep the smile from creeping over my face.

Our little gambit has been underway for almost two weeks, and we've managed to convince quite a few people we're the real deal. For those that know us especially well, the ruse appears to be holding.

Why or how we've managed to snow so many people is a mystery to me. Not that I'm particularly interested in exploring it at the moment. All that will do is lead me down a rabbit hole I'd rather not travel right now. Like Emily said in the beginning—we'll cross that bridge when we get there.

Thank goodness, Shirley wasn't someone we had to work

hard to convince. She's a sweet lady with hair that defies gravity and any known color I could ever recognize. And I get the sense that under that bewildering 'do isn't much in the way of brains. But with all that charm, she doesn't really need them.

She's worked the diner counter since before anyone I know was born. Countless days on the job, but from the look on her face, I'd say we made this one special for her. She just seemed thrilled to see young love (or a facsimile of it) and gave us our fries on the house.

And I have to admit, as much as the idea of this whole charade repelled me at first, I've kind of been enjoying it. After all, I'm spending most of my waking hours with my crush. What's not to like?

Maybe the lack of the actual relationship part?

And let's not forget the missing, more physical part of a romantic relationship. Being close to her like this puts the latter detail in high relief.

Whenever Emily is near, my body is painfully aware of these missing factors.

Even now as we turn into an alley that links to the main street, I shake my head to try and clear my mind.

God, she looks good tonight. Who am I kidding? She always looks good.

These thoughts aren't helping.

And Emily's cute outfit is like some kind of strategic sabotage. Her laughing eyes sparkle at me through the soft glow of the streetlights. It's almost enough to make me think this whole thing is more than just some cheap ploy.

Almost.

"I didn't realize how late it got," Emily says. "We were there for *ages*."

"Well, free fries can make a man pretty giddy."

"Sure can," she replies with a little giggle. "You were positively glowing."

It wasn't the fries, I want to say but bite my tongue.

"Say, how many of these 'dates' are we gonna go on?" I ask instead, half curious, half hopeful.

"I dunno. What's this one? Number six?"

"Seven," I reply, keeping my voice even. I know the exact number, turning each excursion over in my head after I've turned out the light every night. I mean, for a fake couple, we certainly go out an awful lot. And for all these dates, there hasn't been one Leon sighting.

I'm beginning to wonder what this is all about. When, for instance, will Emily do the math and call it off?

Fake or no, I'm not sure how I'd feel about it ending.

Glad I no longer have to pretend? Or sad that even being her fake boyfriend is over?

We reach the end of the alley and suddenly Emily's entire demeanor changes. She stiffens, her eyes shift like a feral cat, and she turns to me, her breathing quick.

"Em? What's up? You okay?" I ask, concern flooding me. That familiar twinge in my heart.

"Leon sighting. Nine o'clock," she says in a terse whisper, her eyes flicking in what I can only guess is the direction of her ex.

Sure enough, I look and spot the dark hulk of him. He's leaning against a parking meter, scrolling on his phone. Perhaps he's waiting to meet someone. If he's fixed his sights on someone else, Emily might let it all slide.

Who cares? A sarcastic voice retorts.

The fact is, our "date" suddenly feels weighted. Like it's suddenly show time.

"Ah. Ok. Yeah. I see him." I squeeze her fingers. It's meant to be reassuring, but all it does is make me think how much I want her to cling to me like this when it's not over some jerk who screwed her up. "What do you want to do? We can just walk by. Or go the other way, or—"

A look overtakes Emily's face, a mix of abject fear and grim determination.

"No, he needs to know. He needs to see. Us. Together. This is what we've been building up to." She sounds like she's giving a pep talk. Whether it's to herself or to me is unclear.

In a flash, Emily throws her head back, her hair cascading over her shoulders in a red waterfall. She lets out a raucous laugh, like she's just heard a raunchy but irresistible joke. I can see her molars, her mouth is open so wide.

Sure enough, her cackle hits the mark. Leon looks up from his phone, searching for the source. I see him clock us, standing the glow of the alley light. As he registers the person laughing, his eyes grow cold.

And then, Emily surprises me. And, if I'm guessing correctly, she certainly surprises Leon.

With a leap, she heaves herself into me, her mouth crashing onto mine.

"Oof…" I exclaim, before the kiss overtakes me completely.

Warmth like lava spreads upwards from my deepest parts, seeping through my limbs.

Her lips are soft; they taste slightly sweet from the ice cream we shared, a tinge of salt from the free fries adding to the aftertaste.

In short, it's a kiss for the ages.

She pulls away, a look of surprise and satisfaction in her expression.

I stare at her, dumbfounded. Leon—and in fact, the whole world—has ceased to exist.

It's only her and me. And the alleyway.

And this moment.

And that kiss.

seven

Emily

Oh my God.
I had no idea.

What started out as a means to trick Leon has become something more. Much more.

Something way beyond Leon.

Kissing Mark is unlike anything I could have expected. A strange spark sizzles in my core, making me look at him with fresh eyes. That single impulsive gesture has made me want only one thing now.

Him.

There's a fire in his eyes that tells me he feels it too. So, I get up on my toes and kiss him again.

Somehow, our mouths know exactly what to do. There is no script to follow. No barriers. No overthinking. My body just naturally responds.

Our mouths, tongues, lips, connect, separate, and reconnect as our breathing syncs. I don't think we could break apart from each other if we tried.

And I don't feel like trying.

My hands move on their own, lifting up from my sides where they've been momentarily frozen. With a shove, I push Mark against the warm, red brick of the alley.

"Ugh," he grunts as air is forced out of him.

"Sorry," I mumble, but we both know I don't really mean it. Something about the aggression of it, the sheer need to let out whatever pent-up feelings I've been holding feels right.

And there's no question we both want it.

Mark's kiss is intense, but not overwhelming. He lets me lead, responding to my lips and letting me guide us until we're matched with equal fervor.

His hands move, his palms spreading out over my sides, my stomach, the small of my back. Every brush leaves my skin radiating with need for more.

They seem to be everywhere. I feel them on my sweater, just underneath the thin jean jacket I'm wearing.

Then, I feel warmth on my breast. Over the sweater, his touch is tender and firm. My skin ignites. It wants more. *So much more.*

My brain can only agree. I press myself against him, feeling the hardness in the front of his trousers for the first time.

Suddenly, Mark pulls away. I almost fall over from his absence, looking up at him with bleary, hungry eyes.

"We… we can't." he mumbles, his lips shining in the dim light, remnants of my recently applied lip gloss. "Not here."

Still breathing hard, I take a second to recalibrate, struggling to get my thoughts back in order.

Right. We can't eat each other alive out here. We'd get arrested. And Cider Mill Valley is far too small for something like that. Word spreads fast, and getting caught in public would haunt us both for the rest of our lives.

"My place," I exclaim, barely able to form more than two words at a time. "It's closer."

He nods and gives me another quick kiss before grabbing my hand. I lead the way, pulling him out of the alley and down the street to where I parked my car.

It's only when I'm fumbling frantically in my purse for my keys—each second I'm not kissing Mark feeling like an eternity—that I realize something.

Leon is gone.

I know he saw us. But when he left, I'll never know.

And right now, I don't care.

The drive home is a blur, a jumbled mix of traffic lights and heavy breathing. Neither of us speak. Hell, I don't even think I can form words. Especially when Mark puts his hand on my thigh, sending sparks shooting upwards. The gentle pressure of each finger only makes me more impatient to get home.

When we finally stumble into my apartment, my whole body is on fire.

"Come in. Make yourself—" I don't finish the sentence. Hell, I don't even flick on the lights. Mark's mouth finds mine, smothering me in hungry kisses.

But this time, there are no prying eyes. No Leons or Shirleys to witness.

Just us. And whatever this is crackling to life between us.

Who am I kidding?

Desire.

Our hands take over. I'm not even sure what belongs to me or to him, and it doesn't matter. All I feel is heat, need, pleasure…

Half stumbling, half moving under some unknown power, we manage to slam my apartment door and travel across the meager excuse for a foyer until we tumble onto my couch.

It's not a fancy thing, just a thrift store purchase, but it's got one fantastic feature. It's long enough to stretch out on. And boy, do we do just that.

Still kissing, Mark lowers me onto the mustard velour

surface, shimmying himself to the edge of the couch, coming to rest on his knees.

It's only then that he stops, takes a sharp breath in and looks at me, brushing some wayward strands of hair from my face.

"I can't believe…" he drifts off, not able or willing to finish his thought.

I don't want him to. I simply want to be in this moment. To have Mark's lips on mine.

Mark.

My always there, always reliable friend.

If I think about it too much…

Cupping Mark's face with both hands, I bring him back to me, engulfing him in a kiss. His words get lost as we dive right back in, our hands resuming their eager explorations. He fumbles his glasses off and slips them on the side table, then doubles down on kissing my neck. That really gets my blood flowing, and I start snatching at his back to keep him there.

Within seconds, I've pulled up Mark's shirt up, jettisoning it over his head. His hair rumples immediately, which is absolutely adorable with his aw-shucks eyes and crooked smile.

In return, he does the same, my sweater sailing off to some unknown corner. I gasp the instant I feel Mark's hands on my bare skin. So warm and sure. Steady and gentle.

Just like him.

My hands slide up and down Mark's chest and back—the skin smooth and taut. He's so slim. I never really noticed Mark's physique until recently. Now that I can finally see it, *feel* it, I'm dumbfounded. Lean and ropey, perfectly toned. Under all those flannel shirts and good boy overlay, he's got quite the body.

"Mmmm… let me…" Mark mumbles, bringing his head into my chest. I run my hands through his hair, closing my eyes to the world as he nuzzles my breasts. The prickle of his stubble stings my skin to life until I'm ready to faint.

Then, with a surprise snap, my bra goes slack and falls away. Mark has, with one hand, flicked the clasp open.

It's one hell of a party trick. My thighs tingle so much I have to press them together.

Mark's mouth meets my bare breast, and I hum in pleasure, his tongue moving around the nipple. My fingers dig into his scalp, his neck, the tops of his shoulders. I feel his skin arch and prickle in response, and his breathing sharpens to tell me how much he likes it.

Then he stops and looks up at me, his eyes drenched in earnest yearning. "May I?" he asks. His husky voice is so plaintive, I shiver.

Part of me is touched by his gentleman-like stance, but the other part just wants him to rip off my jeans. But he looks so tentative I know I have to encourage him to get what my body wants.

Smiling devilishly, I absolve his fears and tear open my fly, pulling my jeans and panties down in a dramatic sweep. Mark's eyes explode wide with wonder and amazement and we both laugh.

But the laughter quickly falls away as Mark gets back to work.

With one hand, he presses my chest to indicate for me to lie down. I don't fight him. How could I? I want this so badly.

Beginning with painstaking care, he starts kissing my kneecaps. It's weird but sweet. At least it would be weird if he stopped there.

Thank God he doesn't.

He kisses his way upward with an agonizing slowness that I both adore and loathe. With each kiss, I get hotter and hotter, my anticipation growing with every light touch of his lips.

I want him there—where the wetness has grown. I want his mouth on me.

But he will not be rushed. No matter how I writhe and whimper, he takes his time torturing me by savoring each taste. I'm powerless to stop him. Lying back, I fling my arm over my face and close my eyes, enjoying each and every one of Mark's attentions.

Then, I feel it—heat right over my secret, warm place. My legs quiver as I ache with need. A silver glint shimmers to life inside me.

For several, eternal seconds, all I feel is Mark's breath. Warm and present. He's making me wait. Making me squirm.

Making me crazy.

It's *divine*.

My hand hovers above his head, all but ready to push his face towards me, when he surprises me again by moving on his own.

Touching me.

Licking me.

"Oh!" I gasp, rocking my head back. The reward for all my waiting is so unbelievably sweet. Sparks fly inside my chest, mini nets of light and heat resounding all through me.

Mark reads every signal my body is sending out. Starting out slowly, he quickly adapts to meet my rhythm. I realize I'm rocking my hips, telling him exactly what I want without my brain saying a thing.

And I know precisely what I want.

How long has it been? How long have I wanted this kind of release? And just how delicious is this way of getting it?

The sparks within me intensify, building up and up, bursting into flames in my blood. My skin is hot, sweat beading up as he teases me closer. It's all brimming to the surface, the fire ready to explode into something else...

Fireworks.

Mark and I move in perfect sync, his mouth answering my

hips. He meets me wherever I am, reading me. It's so sublime I could almost pass out. But I'd never forgive myself if I missed a single second of this. The bonfire grows and grows, crackling upwards until I lose all grip on myself and melt into…

"Jesus, Mark!"

I'm overtaken by that sweet nothingness that comes with release. The abandonment of thought, of worry, of anything this world holds. I'm suspended in pure sensation, untethered to anything resembling thought.

It's glorious.

Shivering and quaking, I slowly come back to earth, my arched back reconnecting with the couch. Mark has pulled back, his eyes sparkling, his mouth slick. He smiles at me, face glowing with pride and affection.

"That was something else," he says.

"Yeah," I whisper. "It really was. Thank you for giving it to me."

Mark grins even more. "I assure you, the pleasure was entirely mine."

This time, I grin. "Really? Here I was eager to see how I could return the favor. Let's see…"

I pull him towards me, my hands finding his jeans, pulling the fly open. Mark obliges, shimmying out of them in no time. He glides over me on the sofa, the heat and closeness of his body making my insides dance. My post-orgasmic warmth mingles with his smooth and silky body, and I hum with appreciation. Our bodies magically fit together, perfectly aligned.

Mark's face hovers above mine, his eyes searching into my soul. For what, I don't know, but I lean back and surrender to his gaze. He ducks close and kisses me. Deep and slow. I taste myself on his lips. My hands rest on his back, the muscles rippling and rolling beneath the skin as I pull him closer.

This feels like madness, but I give up any rational thought.

Then he enters me, slow and sure, chasing my breath high into my chest. He moves with confidence, knowing just how far and how fast to go.

He groans in pleasure, and I answer him right back. The feel of him is exquisite—filling me in just the right way. Scratching an itch I never knew I had.

My legs move to wrap around him, allowing him to take me in even more, deepening our connection.

"God, Emily," he moans. "You feel…" Words trail off and he kicks into high gear. It's exactly what I needed, and I'm only too pleased to match him.

Within moments, we go from slow, lingering movement to rapid, passionate thrusts. Mark's body bucks and undulates, and I meet him with eager hips.

Closing my eyes, I take in his scent—woodsy, clean. Like a walk through a forest. It's every bit as calming as his lovemaking is dizzying.

Moving faster, Mark finds my mouth again. Gentle pecks melt into scalding, ravenous kisses. I can't tell which fuels things more—what's going on below or what's going on with our mouths.

Does it matter?

It all ignites the fire.

We dissolve into a blur of bodies and skin, sweat and sensation. Then, with a shuddering plunge, I feel Mark tense.

"Oh God… Emily, I think I'm…" he stutters.

Then, he's gone, off on his own journey of delicious nothing, glorious absence.

I close my eyes and ride the wave with him, savoring this gift we've given each other.

As what? Friends?

I push those thoughts away and order myself to live in the present. It's simply too good to ruin.

A second later, Mark slackens and collapses onto me, his legs splaying out.

Who could have imagined this couch would fit us both so well?

"Thank you," Mark says, his voice low and breathy. "That was… incredible."

"Yeah. It really was," I reply.

And it was. Truly.

As the moments pass and our breathing slows, I wonder what this all means. What happens now? What do we…

I search my mind for those nagging doubts. Those intrusive thoughts that will tell me I've messed up. Ruined a good thing.

But have I?

Do I have to think about that right now?

My immediate answer lies in the right-now. In the form of a warm and handsome man. Someone who actually gives a damn about me. Whether it's just as a friend or something more is impossible to untangle just now. And yet, suddenly, it's an easy decision to make.

Mark's breathing slackens and slows, and I know he's asleep. The weight of him is strangely delicious. I feel safe beneath him and decide to join him. Within seconds, I'm gone, our bodies cooling on the secondhand sofa.

eight

. . . .

Mark

That *really happened. Right?*

I look around, noting the velvety lilac light that streaks across the open sky. Smell the fresh morning breeze. It's just after dawn.

Taking a deep breath, I note this feeling. I've parked here a million times. This small, squat space outside of my all-too-familiar apartment building. And yet, somehow things look different. Fresher. Everything is just a little bit sharper.

I tell myself it's easy to figure out why. This is not a time when I'm usually awake.

But here I am. Here's my key sliding into my lock, my wrist fiddling with it in the precise way that took me ages to master because the thing is so damn finicky.

The tumblers click and I step into my apartment, the discombobulated feeling drifting right along with me.

It happened?

Yes, it happened. I slept with Emily.

I've dreamed about it so many times I have to keep

pinching myself to make sure I'm actually awake. But this was no dream. Because actually holding her like that was a billion times more powerful than anything I could have imagined.

And I am only just getting home, my clothes infused with the smell of last night's fries and something else—the smell of Emily's apartment. Her skin. Her hair.

Because, yes, I was really there.

It wasn't a dream. Or a vision.

I note the dust motes swirling in the air from being disturbed. The way the egg-yolky light filtering through my need-to-be-washed windows highlights all the housecleaning I always somehow neglect.

It's all still there. It's all still the same. Familiar. My things where I put them. The mail I need to deal with on the side table. The laundry I need to put away on a living room chair. Exactly as I left it.

Except it isn't.

Everything looks slightly different. Like a bizarro version of my former life.

Everything has a sheen to it. A patina. All the usual things are just a touch shinier than they were before.

Because of what happened last night.

I feel like a dunce repeating this in my head, but I can't stop myself. It's all so perfect I just want to relive it *over and over again.* There's no telling what will happen now, but somehow, I can't bring myself to worry about it.

I throw my keys next to my mail and shuffle into my small kitchen, moving on autopilot to make a pot of coffee. Within seconds, the rich smell drifts over me and I stretch my neck muscles, slightly bent and kinked because of where I slept last night.

Where *we* slept.

A thrill races through me. Despite being bone-tired, it happens anyway, starting in my heels and rippling through my whole frame. Because I spent the night in Emily's arms. On her somewhat saggy, lumpy, but utterly perfect couch.

The beep of my coffee maker brings me back to the present and I grab my favorite—if slightly chipped—mug. I don't even bother to put milk in. Or sugar. This morning it's just straight-up caffeine.

As I lift it to my lips, the aroma mixes with something else. Something sweet. Vanilla. Or flowers. Or a summer's day.

I put the mug down and sniff my shirt sleeve.

It smells like her.

Mini-movies of last night cascade across the screen in my mind, waking up all parts of me. My heartbeat thump-thumps in my chest, and my toes tingle. I savor each image as it whips past, even closing my eyes to better saturate myself in them. Hoping I get lost. Hoping it creates a time machine to whisk me back to the instant our bodies met.

A bird squawks outside, a bleating hoot. My eyes fly open, and I feel the grittiness of them. The lack of sleep.

Today's gonna be weird. Long. Possibly hard to get through. It's less than three hours until I have to be at the bookstore.

And Emily will be there.

How can I possibly look at her without longing? Without wanting to jump her in the stacks? Until last night all this was supposed to have been an act, but now? There's no hiding that I've meant every bit of it.

I still do.

But will she feel the same way?

Hard to tell, and thinking it stops me in my tracks.

When I slipped out this morning, we were shy with each other. Our eyes slightly averted, the activities of only a few hours before already becoming nebulous. Memories. Memories that I want to hold onto, relive.

Does she?

Or did I misread things entirely? The coy shyness of her curved body could just as easily have been shame and regret. And the meek kiss on the cheek she gave me as a goodbye? Suddenly all the sparkly feelings in my gut dim.

Bringing the mug back up to my lips, I take a long sip. The hot liquid burns slightly, singeing the back of my throat. I should have given it another second, or taken a smaller sip.

But I didn't. I rushed ahead without thinking. Impatient to be fully awake to tackle what's next. Because what is next, exactly?

There's no going back. Not for me, anyway. I can't forget what happened. I can't just pretend we're just friends anymore. For me, there is no 'back to normal.'

If there's a possible future with Emily, I want to pursue every bit of it. Because she's worth it. More than anyone I've ever known in my life

The trouble is, I don't know if she feels the same.

I take another sip, leaning hard against the kitchen counter. Staring blankly around the room, the one rapidly browning banana on my kitchen table is a grisly reminder that I need to get groceries. My everyday life will keep right on rolling regardless of how the chips fall. It stings to think what happened last night was just a fluke, and I'll be right back to my lonely little world.

We didn't change the terms of our so-called contract. I'm still her *fake* boyfriend. Her blind against Leon.

It's a sobering thought. Remembering Leon and the whole charade behind what pushed us into each other's arms. Downing my coffee in one blistering gulp, a nagging question pulls at me.

When Leon's job in Cider Mill Valley ends, is that the end of this ruse? Is that the end of us? The definitions of our agreement have always been murky and confused. I've longed for clarity from the start, but now I *need* it.

Suddenly urgent, my hand slides into my pocket for my phone.

I want to reach out to Emily, ask her outright what to expect when I walk into the shop today. My thumb hovers over the text message screen, ready to hammer out this all-important question.

Chill, Mark, I tell myself. *Just... wait.* The voice in my head is deep and steady. Rational. Boring, at times.

But now I need to pay attention.

Now is not the time for an interrogation. Especially via text. So much is missing when it's just little bubbles full of vague words. Besides, it's barely 6 am.

This conversation requires more delicacy than I can muster at the moment, and I'm sure Emily would agree with me on that at least. Delicacy should never be handled via text message.

I can't let it go, though. My thumb itches to type something. Best to stick to the mundane. Just let her know I'm here and thinking about her. So, I pluck out the following message:

> Good morning. Made it home safe. See you in a few.

The words look so spare. Should I use an emoji or something? And if so, what? A sleepy face? A sun? A cup of coffee?

A heart?

The thought scares me and I press send before I can let myself make a disastrous error. Turning the phone face-side down, I leave it on the counter and head to the shower.

I've got a whole day ahead. Best to meet it cleanly in every way I can.

nine

. . .

Emily

"How about… a book a day keeps the doctor away?" I ask, biting my lip. My thumb incessantly clicks the top of a pen I'm clutching.

Mark gives me a look, his eyebrows arching.

"Emily…" There's a gentle, almost mocking scold in his voice. He glances between my face and my clicking safety blanket. "The pen? We've been over this." He tries to maintain a stern look, but I can tell he's trying not to laugh.

"Ugh," I groan, smacking it flat on the counter and cringing out a sheepish smile. "Sorry. Yes, I hear you. We have been over this but when I'm thinking a lot, I need to fidget."

"And I hear you. Clicking that dang pen." He finally lets himself laugh before he continues. "Don't think too hard. It'll come to us," he reassures me.

Our boss has left us in charge of coming up with a marketing strategy to promote the bookstore in the upcoming Spring Street Festival. Mostly I think she doesn't want to be bothered, but I secretly suspect she knows we'll do a better job.

"I know. I know," I mumble, trying not to gnaw my cuticle in lieu of clicking my pen. "But time's running out, babe." He gives another look. And I look back. An easy smile grows between us.

I just called him babe, didn't I? Where did that come from?

He says nothing and returns to his thoughts, scribbling down half-baked ideas on a yellow notepad.

"So far, we got… 'spring into books.' Or 'get rooted in a good book' and… your idea."

"That's it?" I ask, somewhat deflated. "I thought we had more."

Mark shrugs. "Hey. You're the creative one, remember? Those cards you make are so cute. But honestly, I think it's enough. Besides, if we're all on our own on this, let's just pick something and go with it. We still have to make all the signs. With your imagination, we could make any one of these work once we start sketching things out."

Something in my stomach flutters at his little compliment about my card making business but I push it away. Considering the ideas for a second, I realize my thumb is desperately trying not to click the pen.

"Let's go with the rooted thing. Feels more springy." I say this with as much conviction as I can muster.

Mark's face grows into a big smile.

"Great! That's the one I wanted too."

My mouth falls open and I swat at him.

"Why didn't you say so?" I keep swatting and he snickers like crazy. "Why all the guessing?"

Mark evades my swipes, playfully running away.

"More fun that way!" He disappears into the back room of the store and emerges moments later with his arms laden with scraps of plywood, cardboard, and various art supplies.

"You dummy!" I rush over to try and take some of it. "Let me help with that!"

"I got it." He laughs again, dumping the loot onto a large table just behind the counter. It's midafternoon and the place is empty, typical for a weekday. Normally I'd be bored senseless, but today I'm pretty grateful. Not just because it gives us a chance to work on the sign in peace. It gives Mark and I a chance to find our equilibrium after… what happened.

"How many people show up to this thing?" Mark asks, as I help him make sense of the markers, scissors, and other supplies scattered about.

"A lot, actually. It's a pretty big deal here in Cider Mill Valley. We get a lot of foot traffic."

"Well, then." Mark squints sideways at the crafting stuff. "Let's hope a catchy sign helps bring 'em in."

"Yeah…" I bite my lip in resignation, realizing the enormity of what we're taking on. "Annette says she makes at least a quarter of her nut from this one weekend alone. I guess we'd better make it good."

Mark flashes another of his patented grins. "With the two of us working on it? You know we will."

I smile back, a dash of wonder bubbling in my chest. Things are so easy with him. Carefree.

Why shouldn't they be?

The question brings me up short.

The night we spent together, only days ago, flashes through my mind. It hasn't happened since and we haven't really talked about it, but strangely there's no whiff of awkwardness, no clouds of doubt or regret hanging between us.

If anything, we are more at ease with each other than ever, laughing and joking our way through our shifts just like before. Maybe even more so.

If it ain't broke…

Unbelievably, an hour later, we've got a template built—a sapling growing from the pages of a book, the words of our slogan swirling upward. I have to admit I'm impressed with how the idea has come together.

"Cute!" I exclaim, impressed by Mark's artistry and patience as we hashed out the details.

"Time to get it cut," he announces, taking the cardboard template outside. Within moments, he's brought out a jigsaw and two sawhorses—from where I have no idea—and traces out the shape in a large piece of plywood.

"Are these your tools?" I ask, squinting in the early spring sunshine. I'm a little cold, the winter chill still lingering, so I clutch my arms around my middle.

Mark winks, the pencil clamped between his teeth making him look handsome and almost rugged.

"Yup. Never get to use them much so I'm happy to do it. Now, put these on and hold this in place?" He hands me a pair of plastic goggles. Great, big, ridiculous goggles. I just know I'm gonna look foolish in them. I give him a sideways look. He smirks.

"Safety first," he drawls, hitting the trigger of his jigsaw so the blade whirrs. But he doesn't move to start actually cutting, so I know he's serious. With a huge, exaggerated sigh, I put them on and station myself at the other end of the plywood.

"Hold her steady," Mark instructs, pulling the trigger again. A high-pitched whine slices through the brisk morning, and within moments Mark has cut out our shape. Powering down, my ears ring from the loud buzz of metal and wood. A voice breaks through the echo.

"You two are just the cutest. Look at you working together. In today's world, it's just nice to see young people getting along."

Old Mrs. Carter has stopped to watch us work. She's a widow, famous in Cider Mill Valley for her Christmas jams and jellies, as well as her quick wit and sharp eyes. She stands, clutching her little purse, her grocery trolley nearby.

"Awww, thanks, Mrs. Carter," Mark says.

Is he blushing?

"We're just… we like working together," he stammers, his eyes glued to the pavement. Even after the time we've spent pretending to be a couple in public, now that things have shifted, we're both quick to blush. I know for sure my cheeks are pink when Mrs. Carter reaches over and touches my arm.

"I know a good one when I see it, sweetie. My Harold was like that. You hold on to this one." Before I can say anything, she rolls her cart away, her peach coat practically glowing in the sunshine.

I catch Mark's eye. His face is inscrutable, slightly in the shadow of the store awning.

Then he smiles.

"You hear that?" he says.

I smile back.

"Sure did."

We don't say another word. We don't have to. A silence falls, but it's not awkward. Just… present.

After a beat, we return to the sign. There's still so much to do.

ten

. . .

Mark

"**D**ang it. Knew I should have measured again before cutting," I mumble to myself, looking at the makeshift backing I've built to hold up the massive sign we've just made. I don't fancy myself a carpenter by any stretch of the imagination, but I thought I'd done a better job than this. Guess I was too busy goofing off with Emily while we were building our display. It's easy to get caught up with her like that.

My dad's voice, slow and reedy, echoes in my ear—*measure twice, cut once.*

"Yeah, Yeah, Dad. I hear ya," I reply through gritted teeth. Dad *was* handy, right up until cancer took him away. Quiet and a little withdrawn, he still had glimpses of warmth to let me know he cared. A good dude, all in all. Even if he rises up to haunt me whenever I'm playing with power tools.

I pull out a measuring tape, trying to figure out if I can shore up the backing a little. Lord knows I wouldn't want this thing falling apart during the festival and toppling on someone. That would definitely *not* be good for business.

Gritting a pencil in my teeth and doing some quick math in my head, I'm about to head back into the store to get more tools when a voice stops me.

"You like books *and* power tools, huh? What are you, a Medieval Times kinda guy?"

My brain does a double take.

Yes, that's Leon.

But that's only part of what trips me up. It actually takes me a moment to work out his attempted reference.

"Do you mean a *Renaissance* man?" I ask.

Leon shrugs, his eyes clouding over in annoyance.

"Sure. Whatever. Yeah. Look, I'm just making small talk, okay?" Leon says, curtly. He doesn't exactly seem the type that likes to be corrected. Or have it pointed out that he's pretty stupid.

I make a mental note.

I take a breath and make a decision. I can either be a dick to this guy, or I can play nice and get him to leave. Quickly, if I do it right.

"Oh yeah. Cool. Just building a little something for the Spring Festival. Boss wants something—"

Leon waves a hand and cuts me off.

"Yeah, yeah. Look, is Emily here?" He cocks his head to one side, scanning the store window.

A curl of hair falls from his well-gelled head. Why does it piss me off so much that I can see why women might go for someone like this? He has a whole roguish James Dean thing going on. God knows I could never pull that off even if I wanted to. Which I don't. It's still something I have always hated in others.

"Uhhh." I shrug and look over my shoulder at the shop. "No, not yet. She'll be along at some point though."

Please be late, please be late, I wish to whomever might

control these things. The last thing I need is for Leon, Emily, and I to wind up having to make small talk out in the street.

Leon nods, like I've told him something meaningful.

"How's she… uhhh… how's she doing?" I blink. The question feels false somehow. Searching. Like he really wants to ask something else. Something far more pointed but he doesn't have the balls to come out and ask it.

"She's fine. Great, in fact," I reply. A hint—only a hint, mind you—of smugness creeps into my voice. Is it possible I'm making this dimestore Lothario stew?

A flash of the night I spent with Emily steals across my mind. It never fails to give me a thrill. Deep inside. Seeing her head thrown back… her lips parted… the sheen of sweat on her…

Leon nods but I can't tell what info is making him do that. He looks like he wants to ask me something else.

"Listen, man…" Turns out he does. Leon leans a little closer and drops his voice. "I'm just curious—"

Before he can finish, another voice breaks through.

"Isn't it weird when two people you don't expect to find in the same place… just *are*?" Looking past Leon, I catch sight of Emily's friend Samantha strolling up. Well, maybe not her *friend*. Emily has confessed to me more than a few times Samantha is more of a 'frenemy'.

Samantha is something else. A petite blonde with ice-blue eyes and shiny white teeth, she could be considered attractive if her personality wasn't so jarring. To me, at least. Plenty of guys get dazzled by her looks and don't seem to notice the rest.

She stops near Leon and I, putting her hand on her hip as she studies us. Emily isn't far behind her, a mixture of surprise and worry crossing her face before she hides it behind a smile.

"Hi, you two!" I say, a little too cheerily. I'm always happy to see Emily, but I could do without the others. We all stand staring at each other, the most awkward quartet ever, before Samantha breaks it.

"Looks like a parade of Ken dolls." *Can always count on good ol' Sam to have a thought.* "Just for you, Emee. Your whole collection is here."

She lobs out this bomb along with a nickname I know Emily hates. One thing about Samantha—she doesn't have a filter. Anything that pops into her head is immediately funneled right out of her mouth. At best her thoughts are plain annoying, and at their worst, downright toxic.

Leon's eyes flick from me to Emily and back again. I can feel him sorting out the details in his head.

That kiss. I know he saw that kiss. Emily made sure he did. But what else does he know? Has our ruse fooled him? Have the local gossips been doing their good deeds?

"Haha, yeah," Emily says lamely, trying to fill the gaping hole Samantha's comment left in its wake. Her body language suggests that all she wants to do is either disappear into a puddle on the pavement, or claw Samantha's eyes out. I can't tell quite which. But I know which I'd prefer.

Leon nods, then makes a little grunting sound.

"Well. Yeah. This has been fun but..." He trails off and gives the two of us another look before mumbling, "Gotta go." With that he turns to head down the street.

"Wait!" Samantha calls. "Where you headed? I was just walking our cutie little Emee to work, but now I'm off to run a few errands. Want to go with me?"

Her voice is so treacly sweet it's almost cloying. I try to suppress a shudder. Leon on the other hand turns back and eyes up Samantha, assessing her like a fox stalking prey.

"Uhh, yeah." That I-don't-care cool-guy look slips over his face again. "Sure, you can walk with me for a bit."

Samantha beams like she's won a pie-eating contest and weaves her arm through his before he even knows what's happening.

"That sounds *perfect*. See you, Emee. Try to behave…" She winks at Emily and gives me a smile with frost behind her eyes. She knows I don't like her. Turns out the feeling is mutual.

Okay by me.

Moments later, they've meandered out of sight down the street.

The whole dreadful encounter lasted less than five minutes but it felt like a decade. Emily turns to me, almost green with discomfort.

"Sorry, Mark. That was…"

I shrug, trying to make light of the situation.

"Don't worry about it. Samantha is only trying to—"

"She's the worst," Emily growls before I can finish. "I don't know why I keep hanging out with her. And Leon? What the hell was he doing here?"

"Not sure." I shrug again. My shoulders are getting a workout today. "I think he was trying to get some info about you, but I'm not sure what his whole deal is."

"Yeah." She nods for a second, biting her lip. The way she does it, it's all I can do not to kiss her. Then she looks up at me and asks, "Think it's working?"

The question stings.

I don't want this ruse to be just that. A ruse. Nothing more. Hell, it's already more to me. But I can't say anything. I know what I agreed to. Our little fling the other night notwithstanding, I got roped into playing a part in all this.

"Maybe," I say, turning back to the sign. "I should get back to this. It's not going to fix itself." Emily stands for a beat, but I can't bring myself to look at her.

"Thanks, Mark. I'll see you in there?"

"Yup. Give me a few," I reply, trying to hide my face. Emily sighs and pauses. It's clear she's waiting for me to do something, but I'm weirdly disinclined. But the moment stretches on, and she doesn't head inside.

I can't help it. I have to ask.

"You okay?"

"Yeah," she replies. "Just..." She nudges the edge of our sign with her toe.

"What?" I prod.

"I *hate* being called Emee!"

That shatters the moment, and we both fall out laughing. Some of the tension ebbs away, and I can't help thinking maybe the day will get better now. Given how things started, it'd be hard to get worse!

eleven

. . .

"**Y**ou be careful, now," calls Mr. Grimshaw.

"Don't you worry about me. I'll be fine," I say, in the singsong tone I only use with him. The former town pharmacist keeps an almost permanent vigil at the north end of the main street. Everyone in Cider Mill Valley knows good and well that Grimshaw just isn't good at being retired.

I suppose being the eyes and ears of everyone's business for years would be hard to let go of. He's harmless, though and I don't mind throwing a word or two his way as I pass by him on my way home. Just thinking it might brighten his day often lifts my spirits as well.

Tipping up my chin, I take a deep breath of the fragrant, early evening air. After that weird interaction outside the bookstore with Leon and Samantha, the day hummed along. It's funny how much comfort I can take in things being unremarkable. Lord knows there's plenty to get me mixed up.

For once, I've decided to stick to my plan of actually going home and catching up on chores. The laundry alone is enough to make my head spin.

"No date tonight?" Mark asks as we get ready to head down separate streets to our separate apartments.

"Not tonight. I've got loads to get done." I shoulder into him, nudging his upper arm. "I bet you do too." For a second, I think I see disappointment flicker across his face, but he quickly recovers.

It could have been a trick of the light, I say to myself. What does it even matter? We've been working pretty hard at this ruse thing. Probably best to take a break.

"Shucks." Mark chuckles. "Looks like it's just me and my crosswords tonight then."

"Well, yeah. Don't want to let that go for too long. Your brain will get mushy." It's funny, but I get a queasy feeling in the pit of my stomach picturing him alone in his apartment, busy with his pen under the lamp. I'm almost tempted to say my laundry can wait but think better of it. Best not to let my emotions get the best of me.

"Anyway," he says softly. "I'll see you tomorrow."

"Yeah." We hug goodnight.

It's longer hug than our usual hugs. Well, longer than the hugs we used to give each other before…

Before the night we shared.

Something in my body thrums at his touch but I squish it down. I need to focus. I need to get on with my ever-growing to-do list.

Not only that—I need some space to sort out my thoughts. They've been jumbled lately, to say the least.

A night at home on my own will do me good, I remind myself.

"Night," I say as casually as I can muster, pulling out of the hug. "See you in the morning."

"Yup, yup," Mark replies, his voice slightly higher than usual.

Before I can think about it too much, I head off in the

opposite direction, throwing an extra wave Mr. Grimshaw's way. But he's not the only person I encounter on my walk home.

"Emeeeeee," comes a drone from somewhere off to my side. I manage to stifle my shudder just in time before Samantha manifests in front of me.

"Samantha! Hi! Where are you coming from?" Now it's my turn for my voice to be unnaturally high. Something about her makes me nervous every time I'm around her.

Samantha looks coquettish—a mask she has to pull on because it's so far from her natural state.

"Oh me? Just leaving Bardo's. Had dinner with…" She pauses, as if waiting for an expected drumroll of anticipation. "Leon!" She clamps her hands on her hips, blocking my path. Her eyes twinkle. She's searching my face for a reaction. Something to tell her… *anything*, I suppose? I'm not sure what she's going for.

Thankfully, I manage to keep my expression blank. I'm determined not to give anything away.

"Oh? Nice. I haven't been there yet. Saving up."

Bardo's is the newest spot in Cider Mill Valley and seems to be determined to give Nona Bella a run for its money in the fine dining department. It's all cloth napkins and steak rather than burgers.

But hey, fancy is in the eye—and stomach—of the beholder.

My attention drifts past Samantha for a mere second and she pounces.

"Don't worry. He left already. He had to go. But he picked up the tab, so I didn't mind." Seemingly satisfied she's discovered something in my expression, she stops blocking my path and coils her arm through mine.

An irritating, sisterly gesture she always initiates. I don't know if she's ever noticed I never do.

"I'll walk you home," she says, her voice pretending to be

sultry. "We live so close, I'm surprised we don't do that more often."

"Yeah… me too," I say, though I know the real reason only too well. Often, I'll plan my walks home for times when I know she might be at work.

I'm being petty, aren't I?

Samantha is okay, I suppose.

In *small* doses.

We start moving, and Samantha controls the speed of our steps so we're walking in perfect tandem. It's uncanny how she always manages to do that. I stay quiet, doing my level best to keep things light while trying not to talk about anything at all. I figure I have about five minutes before my apartment building comes into view.

I can handle five minutes… unless she chooses to linger on the sidewalk…

"Soooooo, how was your day?" Samantha asks, drawing out the vowels—yet another signature trait of hers.

"Fine. People keep buying books no matter what the robots say. So, I still have a job." I chuckle lamely at my own observation, hoping it will draw her into a conversation about the perils of running a small business, the constant threat of internet retailers dominating the publishing world.

Samantha opens her mouth to reply and any dreams I had of having that conversation go straight out the window. Instead, she veers into the single topic I'm hoping to avoid.

"Leon and I had the *best* time. He really knows how to treat a girl. Cocktails, appetizers, entree, dessert… the works. He's a keeper," she croons. Then, squeezing my arm she says, in what I guess is a playful tone, but it just comes off as conspiratorial.

"But you knew that already, didn't you?"

"Uhhh. I guess. Leon knows how to pay for dinner, if that's what you're getting at," I reply, doing my best to be diplomatic.

Leon is many things—most of them unpleasant—but he was never cheap. His 1950's sense of how men and women should work meant that I knew he'd insist on picking up the check. I argued with him in the beginning but slowly saw the futility of it. The ugly truth I can admit to myself now was that I enjoyed being wined and dined. Just a little. It doesn't mean I owed him my life or anything.

"Oh, come on, he's more than that," she says, slapping my upper arm. "He's a real catch."

I shrug, trying to loosen her vice-like grip on me. "If you say so."

Samantha makes a gasping sound. "If I *say* so? Come on, Emee, you know it. In fact, you know it so much that's why you're making googly eyes at that boring farm boy whenever Leon comes around."

I almost stop short at the characterization. The idea of Mark as a boring farm boy is almost too ridiculous to compute. I force myself to keep walking, trying to keep a lid on my anger.

"Mark is no boring farm boy. Quite the opposite, actually—"

"Oh, please," she cuts in. "He's a thick-skulled, doe-eyed *bore*. I doubt he has two brain cells to rub together. And even if he does, I'm certain he barely has two dollars to rub together. He could never afford to take you out like Leon does."

It takes all my energy to keep things cool. I merely say, "That's your opinion then."

"It *is*! And you want to know another opinion I have?" I open my mouth to respond but she plows on. "I think you're just doing that to get Leon back. I see your ploy, Emee. Believe me, I know that game. I practically invented it. You're trying to get Leon back with the oldest trick in the book. Have to say, I didn't peg you for that type, but I guess all women can play that game when they want to."

She punctuates her little courtroom closing statement with a prim smile and stops walking.

By some miracle, we've arrived right outside my apartment. She had me seeing red so much I hadn't even noticed us getting close. I'm both elated we're finally here and bristling with anger at her callous and shallow observations. All the same, I hold my tongue. I don't want her to know any of that.

"Well, here we are," I say, slipping my arm from hers. "Thanks for walking me home, Samantha. Glad you had a good time with Leon."

I turn to head up the path to the front door, but Samantha catches me by the sleeve.

"It makes me feel better, you know?" she says. I cock an eyebrow at her. What's she talking about now? "That you're one of us. I used to think you were above me somehow, like a better person? But no, you're catty like me. I *love* it. Anyway, 'night!"

She saunters off into the velvety darkness, her white skirt glowing as she sways her hips. Samantha always knows how to make an exit. I stare at her sashaying down the street until she's long gone. An acid sting in the back of my throat begs me to scream something after her, but I can't think of anything nasty enough.

Fiddling with my keys, I try to make sense of our conversation.

Have I really been trying to make Leon jealous this whole time? To what end? So, he would beg me to come back to him? Maybe some part of me always wanted that but when I think about it now, it's like trying to grasp at the wind. It just flies through my fingers. I don't want him back at all. In fact, that's the last thing I want.

He and Samantha can have all the dinners they like together. He could spend his life savings taking that woman out to dinner and it wouldn't bother me in the least. In fact, when I think about who I want to spend my time with, only one face pops into view. Only one face makes my heart skip a beat.

Mark.

My key slides into the front door lock as it hits me.

"Wait," I mutter to myself. "Am I in love with Mark?"

A tiny voice in my core replies without hesitation.

Yes.

Holy crap, I'm in love with Mark. Utterly and truly.

A heady mix of fear and elation courses through my veins, and I rush to my apartment, desperate to sit down.

On the mustard couch. Where it all happened.

Memories bum-rush me, clouding my vision.

I'm in love with Mark.

It's indisputable.

But that definitely wasn't part of the plan.

Not part of the plan at all.

twelve

. . .

Mark

"**D**id you see the new shipment came in?" I ask, dabbing the corner of my mouth with a napkin. "Bet that bestseller is in there. The one everyone's been calling about? Who knows? We might have a rush on our hands." I chuckle softly, but Emily doesn't respond. She merely spoons some more chicken noodle soup into her mouth and stares into the middle distance. A knot forms in my stomach, and I lock my face into what I hope is a friendly, carefree expression.

What is going on? She's acting so weird today.

"Emily?" I prod, "penny for your thoughts?"

She looks up, startled, as if she's just discovered she's in a diner. With me. On our lunch break.

"Sorry! My mind is goofy today, I guess." She swirls her spoon in her soup as if she's playing a game of tag with the pieces of chicken. Noodles and carrots float around in lazy circles, bumping into each other. It doesn't look like anything to me, but Emily stares at it like she's trying to read tea leaves or something.

"That's okay," I assure her. "Happens to the best of us. Anything I can help with?" I pluck a fry from my plate and pop it into my mouth. Partly because I'm famished and partly to keep me from rambling. Or rather, asking her a barrage of awkward questions.

"No, I'm okay," she replies, giving me a smile that doesn't quite reach her eyes.

"Okay." Much as I'd like to prod some more, I force myself to leave well enough alone. For the last two days, Emily has been *different*.

Aloof. Cagey, even.

At the same time, I don't get the vibe that she wants to avoid me. Quite the opposite. It seems that she's…

Staring at me? Giving me really intense looks from across the room? a voice says. A voice that I want to believe is true.

Though she's gone quiet, I've caught Emily staring at me more than once over the past two days. Her eyes are always searching—almost *probing*. Like she's trying to work out a really intense puzzle in her head.

Is it possible I'm that puzzle?

It feels like too much to hope all these lingering looks are about something more. That maybe she's started to feel what I've felt since I first met her.

Sitting across from me now, however, her eyes are everywhere *but* on me. Which is less than ideal. And damn sure punctures my wishful little theory.

Time to switch tactics.

"Here. You gotta have some of these sweet potato fries. I can't eat 'em all," I propose, holding out a fry across the table.

For a frighteningly long moment, my hand hovers in the air, the fry held like a peace offering. The knot in my stomach grows tighter. Is she going to let me hang here like an idiot? A flush of embarrassment and sadness well up through my chest.

If only she'd…

"Sure," she says, turning those impossibly sparkling eyes on me. It's like getting hit by a sunbeam. Instantly, my sadness ebbs. The frustration flies away.

Is that all it takes? For her beautiful eyes to look my way? I might be even further gone than I realized. A crush is one thing, but this borders on something else. Something far more dangerous if she doesn't feel it too.

She opens her mouth and leans forward to reach the fry. I can't help but notice how her breasts graze the top of the table and how inviting her open mouth is. With about one inch to spare, her eyes meet mine and they are, without a doubt, full of hunger. The same kind of all-consuming hunger that I saw the night she kissed me. The night we did more than just kiss.

Fire erupts in my brain, my heart, my chest. My groin.

This is no accident. Emily is giving me a signal. Pure and simple.

Her perfect teeth surround the fry and pluck it from my fingers with a satisfying snap, and she leans back, chewing slowly.

I stare at her, my mouth hanging open.

Tell her to play hooky with you this afternoon, a voice urges. A sexy, demanding voice.

I lean forward, taking her hand in mine. She smiles, reading my signals instantly. It's no great feat—they're as obvious as sunlight. My body rises from my chair with a will of its own, my face moving towards hers. She's leaning in as well. Our mouths open. I tingle in anticipation of what's about to happen.

Since that one night, we haven't shared anything like this, and I've been hungry to taste her lips again.

A laugh pierces the moment like an icepick. It stutters and collapses, pushing me back into my chair and Emily reeling into hers.

Samantha.

My eyes flick to the right and there she stands, near a

neighboring booth. She's just come in from outside, her cheeks still rosy from the brisk air. Or maybe it's delight at catching us about to kiss.

As usual, her hands are on her hips, her head cocked, a mean-spirited smile on her face.

"You guys are getting better at this," she says. "Really convincing." Her sarcastic words come out like barbs. Emily looks like she's been slapped. Her face grows pale, and her eyebrows shoot up in surprise.

Me? I have a different reaction.

Very different.

It's like a big firecracker set off in a very small room. Rage blooms in my chest and I hear the shriek of metal as I stand up quickly, my chair scraping the polished floor.

"Isn't there *anything* you could be doing right now instead of being a massive pain in the ass?" My voice booms through the diner and every head in the place whips around to see what's going on. The normally sleepy waitress perks right the hell up as well.

I don't care. I just want this menace—this *mosquito*—gone. And I'm ready to get swatting.

Now it's Samantha's turn to be surprised. A startled little breath slips out of her as she takes a step back.

If I've put her off her game, the moment is short-lived, and she immediately regroups.

Bullies are good at that.

"Whoa there, cowboy. Settle down. Haven't you learned it's not nice to talk to a lady like that? Especially here in Cider Mill Valley?"

My teeth grind against each other as I turn to face her head on.

"Sure have. But right now, I'm not talking to a lady. I'm talking to something else entirely." My voice is barely above a growl, and I hear Emily making an 'eep' sound as she hears my words.

I'm not playing around.

Samantha loses her cool again. It's clear I've hit a nerve. Her features curl into a nasty snarl.

"You play the simple, nice boy routine but I know what you really are. A fake. A liar. A stooge for Emily. You know what you are, *Mark*?" She spits my name at me as if it's an insult all by itself. "You're pathetic."

Flames of anger ripple through me and I take a small step towards her. I have no plan, exactly. I just want this to end. But how?

"You okay, Sam?" a voice asks.

I turn my head and realize I have another problem on my hands. One that's a little bigger and a lot more dangerous.

Leon stands in the doorway.

Game on.

My confusion calcifies into rage. I'm not backing down.

Game on, indeed.

thirteen

Emily

This isn't happening, this isn't happening, I repeat to myself
over and over. But there's no getting around it. Mark
and Leon face off like two snorting rams ready to smash into
each other right here in the diner.

"Hey. I asked you a question," Leon barks.

For a moment, nobody moves. I take it as my cue to
intervene. If I'm lucky, maybe I can get ahead of this.

"Uhh… Leon? You asked Sam a question, actually," I
clarify, hoping this will diffuse the mounting tension. All the
diners have turned to face us and the waitstaff has pooled
behind the main counter, leaning forward on their elbows.
Their jaws are slack in fascination. The manager hovers, his
hand near the phone, ready to call the cops if that's what it
comes to. I truly hope it doesn't.

Great. Now my life is an actual sideshow.

My remark only seems to irk Leon. He shifts his weight
and scowls.

"Keep your observations to yourself, Emily," he spits. "I

can smell a bully a mile away. And it seems this pencilneck is pretending to be one."

"You would know," Mark hisses back. "Seems like the only thing you're known for around here is being one yourself. Certainly not known for your intelligence." From the corner of my eye, I see some people nod in agreement. Leon isn't exactly the brightest bulb in the socket.

For her part, Samantha looks like she's dying to pull out the popcorn and play the part of damsel in distress at the same time. In other words, she's not helping the situation whatsoever.

Leon sloughs it off.

"Brains are for the weak. I get by just fine. In fact, right now, I definitely think I have the advantage. What are you, anyway? Just some dishrag bookworm hanging around weaklings all day. Why don't you sit on down, stick your nose in a book, and stop harassing everyone around here?" Leon licks his lips. It's a gesture I've seen before. He's getting ready for a fight.

I slide my eyes to Mark, internally begging him to back down.

Walk away.

Yes, it'll be embarrassing for him, but I know he's no match for Leon. Mark isn't exactly small, but he doesn't have a fighter's bone in his body.

Or does he?

He's certainly proven to be full of surprises up to now. All the same, I keep right on imploring him with my eyes.

If Mark catches my look, he ignores it.

"Not harassing anyone. Just having lunch. But if you're confused about this, why don't we step outside so these fine people can enjoy the rest of their day? I'd love to show you just what I'm capable of."

I've never seen Mark like this. His eyes are ice-cold, and

his hands clench open and shut. His body is practically thrumming.

Leon smiles back. A wicked, cunning smile. Like the predator he is.

"Fine by me, Shakespeare. Let's go."

My hand shoots out to grab Mark's elbow.

"Mark, no. You don't have to do this," I protest but Mark shrugs me off, his eyes locked on Leon's back as he exits the restaurant.

I have no choice but to tag uselessly behind. Samantha can barely conceal a Cheshire cat grin, but as I pass near her, she changes expressions instantly. Now she's all wronged, hurt, and distressed.

"He's so mean to me, you know," she whimpers. Rage ticks up deep in my belly but I ignore it—and her. Instead, I brush past her to head outside. I'll have to deal with her later.

Out on the sidewalk the two men stand a few feet apart, squaring off like bull and matador. I don't want to admit that any sane person would put money on Leon in this fight but my heart roots for Mark.

Well, my heart actually roots for this all to be a nightmare. If only I could pinch myself and stop the whole thing in its tracks.

Please. Wake up. Make this all go away.

I close my eyes for a second but when I open them again, reality hits me with a thud. This isn't a nightmare. It's real.

"Now what, Leon? You seem to know so much. What now, big boy?" Mark taunts, his voice harsh.

I don't like this side of Mark, but I don't have a say in the matter. He's in too far to back up now.

Leon, naturally, is in his element, having had more than his fair share of scraps.

"Here's the part where you learn your place, jackass," he growls. "Where you learn the difference between the men and the boys."

His body language is more relaxed than Mark's. He's in his element here, waiting for Mark to do something stupid. Any little slip-up to give him what he's looking for—a way in.

"Really?" Mark snorts. "Men and boys? This is what you have? Some caveman shit? What are you trying to prove? Sounds like a lot of hot air to me. Maybe that's what you really are, Leon. A lot of hot air, and that's it."

On the surface, it's a good argument. One that any reasonable person would realize and back away from. Too bad for everyone Leon's never been reasonable.

With a sinking feeling, I see that's exactly the moment of weakness that Leon needed.

"I don't have to prove I'm a man. I know it. But if you're confused, just ask Emily. She'll tell you. How I made her scream. How I made her tremble. How I made her so wild with desire—"

Leon's last words are lost behind the haymaker Mark whisks at his head. It's a mean right hook but Leon is more than ready for it. Ducking expertly, Leon shifts his weight and swings his left hand up and around, landing a belter across Mark's face.

The sound of it is almost as bad as seeing it. Mark's completely stunned. It's a real wallop.

Something inside me breaks.

"Stop it!" I shriek. "STOP IT RIGHT NOW!" The voice comes from some deep, unknown source. I sound like a banshee, a wailing woman.

I sound deranged.

And I don't give a damn.

It is enough to break the spell. Mark, looking dazed, stumbles back onto a bench by the restaurant door. Leon smirks, but some of his bravado is diluted, less potent by my outburst.

"Just telling the truth, babe." The bastard actually has the audacity to wink at me before ambling away.

As he does, the whole atmosphere melts into numb, stinging silence.

Such a stupid, needless thing.

I stand stone still, breathing hard, unable to process a single thought or feeling. When I finally get my bearings and look up, Samantha has wisely disappeared.

Mark sits, looking at me, his hand on his chin and his shoulders slumped. He looks bewildered. Sheepish.

"Mark, I…"

My words dry up. What could I possibly say right now? I walk away.

I need space.

I need to think.

I need to get away.

fourteen

Mark

W*hat kind of barbarian shit did I just pull?*
And what kind of idiot sets himself up for an easy punch like that?

Me, that's who.

Primo Idiot Number One.

The area in front of the diner is deserted, but I can feel a crowd of eyes looking at me through the front window. Each one watching the loser standing alone with nothing but his empty threats and ragged pride.

My anger has drained away, replaced by embarrassment and shame.

What the hell was I trying to prove anyway? That I could handle Leon? That I wasn't going to be pushed around by the likes of Samantha?

All I've managed to do is show everyone I'm a prize idiot —and alienate Emily in the process.

That's the bitterest pill to swallow.

I can live with people snickering behind my back, but

humiliating her? That's gonna sting for a long time. A hell of a lot longer than a bruised cheek. Lifting my hand up to prod around—Leon had definitely left a mark—I try to banish the feeling of hurting Emily. Even pushing harder to inflict a little pain on myself as some kind of weak recompense. All it does is leave me more ashamed of myself.

Emily told me to stop. But I couldn't.

My dumbass pride wouldn't let me. And now I don't know if I've actually ruined everything for good.

I have to find her. I have to make things right.

Slinking back inside, I throw some money on the counter to cover our meal and bolt out again as fast as I can. The last thing I want right now is anyone asking me questions. That done, I dash to the only place I think Emily will be—the bookstore.

After all, Emily is nothing if not loyal.

To whom, though?

I ignore the nagging voice as I make my way to the shop, but it only gets louder. By the time I reach the front door it's practically screaming in my skull. The cheery little bell jingling as I shove my way in definitely isn't helping.

Thank God, the place is empty. It makes sense, given we've been closed for lunch break. I'm just relieved because I don't think I could handle small talk right now.

Making my way to the back room, I pull up short just before I step through the door. The sound is soft, but unmistakable.

A woman crying.

My heart clenches.

"It's all right, honey. It was just a brief moment…" Annette's gravelly no-nonsense voice tries to soothe Emily. "Things get out of hand sometimes." It's so weird to hear Annette saying something comforting—she's so straightforward, an arrow would ask her for directions.

But for all her thorny exterior, Annette has a heart of gold and it's clear she cares about Emily.

I push open the door just a bit and catch sight of Emily sitting in a heap on the bar stool by the new shipments. Annette has her hand on Emily's knee, another uncharacteristically tender gesture. By the way she glares at me, however, it's pretty clear I can't expect the same sympathy.

"Hey." My voice is weak, but it sparks the whole room. Annette stands up, putting herself between me and Emily like she's shielding her.

"I don't think this is a good time, do you? Mark, why don't you take the rest of the day—"

I hold up my hand, straining to look past Annette to where Emily is wiping her eyes on her sleeve.

"Annette, please. I just need a minute. I know I messed things up. But I need just a second to explain. Okay?" Words aren't doing much, so I look directly at Annette, imploring her with my eyes.

I just need to talk to Emily. To make her not hate me. To make her understand that I'd do anything for her. Even make a fool out of myself in public. Even with all the shame coiling around my stomach, I would do it again in a heartbeat if it meant Emily would know how much I care about her.

Annette starts to interrupt again, but to my utter surprise, she stops and raises her hand near my bruised cheek.

"You should ice that," she growls and starts to leave. "Let me see what I can find."

"Thanks," I reply, relief flooding me. "I won't take long."

"You better not," Annette says curtly. "We have to reopen."

And with that, she's gone. Leaving me alone with Emily.

I turn to face her, the room shrinking around us. Smaller. Stuffy. The tension palpable.

"Emily, I…" My words abandon me. What can I possibly say? I want to make things right, but is that even possible?

"Why," she asks softly, that single word shattering my heart. "Why'd you do it? You know Leon is a brute." Emily sniffs, her red-rimmed eyes finally lifting to mine.

"I don't know," I confess. "Something in me just snapped and I…" It sounds so stupid. So *petty* as I say it. Emily just shakes her head in disappointment.

"He wanted you to do that. He was playing you. And *everyone* saw." She buries her face in her hands, her shoulders shaking a little.

I step forward, aching to hold her. To be the shoulder she can cry on. The strong guy she needs. The one she deserves.

Instead, I'm the moron who embarrassed her in front of half the town.

And got your ass kicked, that unhelpful voice reminds me.

Taking a deep breath, I start piecing together the jumbled feelings inside me, willing them into sentences.

This is your only shot to make this right.

"I couldn't stand idly by and watch Leon and Samantha talk to you like that. Or say the things about you that he did. In front of everyone like that? What kind of a friend would I be if I let that happen?"

I take yet another step, my skin crying out to touch hers. But that would only frighten her off. The moment is too fragile.

Emily holds her breath, weighing my words.

"I care about you, Emily. So much. I may even—"

I stop myself just short of saying the words. Those three words that can make or break the next moment. They are too powerful right now. Best to walk them back.

"I have feelings for you. Perhaps feelings beyond friendship and I…" I look down at my hands and take a deep breath. "I guess what I'm saying is, I know we built this 'fake' relationship to keep Leon away. And perhaps if you don't *actually* hate me for what happened out there… maybe we could take the 'fake' part out of it?"

There it is.

I said what I wanted without really saying it. Clumsily? Absolutely. But at least where I stand is out in the open.

All I can do now is hope that Emily agrees.

fifteen

...

Emily

"Um. Mark, please… hold on a second," I stutter, trying to get a handle on everything I'm feeling. Which is impossible. Every time I think I can pinpoint one emotion, another rushes in to take its place.

Confusion, shame, anxiety, terror, hope, and most painful of all—love.

I've already admitted to myself I might love Mark, but I'm not ready to face it yet. I certainly have feelings for him. That I can't deny.

"Emily, I just…" He takes a step closer. From the moment he found us back here, he's been inching closer. It's comforting and terrifying at the same time. I have no idea what I'd do if he actually touched me.

Looking at the shining bruise on his cheek, my anxiety really starts to spike. Right or wrong, he earned that for *me*.

"Mark, this whole thing. This whole fake relationship thing…" I hit a cul-de-sac in my brain and my words dry up. What am I trying to say? What do I want right now?

I definitely feel things for him, but he's galloping way ahead of me, and not waiting for me to join him.

Would I, though? Would I agree to taking out the *fake*? That would only leave the *real*. And I'm not sure what's real and what isn't right now.

"Emily, I hope I'm not speaking out of turn, but I really think there's something more here. Something we both feel. I just can't stand by and ignore it any longer. Please."

He takes another step, and I feel the warmth of him, smell his woodsy scent. My brain flashes, lurid and bright, images of his body, or his slightly open mouth as he leans forward to kiss me. It's all so vivid I have to turn away to keep my thoughts in line.

"Mark," I begin hoarsely, licking my dry lips. "I know what we agreed to, and I have to think about whether we should keep it this way. Yes, the times we've had together have been fun, but I don't know if I'm ready for anything more right now. Being with Leon messed me up pretty bad and I'm so grateful you stepped up to play a part. But that's all it was, Mark. Playing pretend. I don't know if we can read any more into it." My heart shrivels at my own words.

It's a lie and we both know it. But who will admit that first?

Mark takes a step back, as if I'd punched him harder than Leon ever could. His eyes roll to the ceiling, a heavy sigh falling out of his chest.

"Bullshit." The word snaps like a whip in the small, dim room. When I look up, he's watching me with an unreadable expression. "Emily, I don't buy that for a second. I know what I agreed to and that's all very well and good, but my heart tells me something else. And I think you see we really have something here. Something real. Something more than a trick. Can we at least try it?"

God, his voice is so sincere. Full of longing. And so much

more than that. If I'm not careful, my shattered heart might just start to repair itself.

Something in me relents and I look harder, trying to read his face. Searching for anything to help me make sense of what I'm feeling. I open my mouth to respond—not even sure what I'm going to say—when another voice cuts in.

"I knew it."

We both swivel sharply to see Samantha standing in the doorway.

How the hell does she do that? Does she have a special signal or something?

Her face is the picture of smug, smiling triumph.

Mark and I are paralyzed, both struck dumb by her presence. How did she even get in here?

"Oh, my *God*," she cackles. "I can't wait to tell Leon. We both suspected all along, but this is too much. You were both playing pretend? How *sad*." Her voice drips with self-satisfied rancor.

And for the first time since this whole day got out of hand, I understand why Mark wanted to pick a fight. Because all I want in the world is to wipe that grin off her face.

"Hey!" Annette's voice blasts from somewhere behind Samantha. "What are you doing here? We're not open yet!"

Samantha turns to our boss and feigns innocence, even clutching her neck to complete the charade.

"Oh! I'm sorry! I saw the door was open and thought I'd come in. And I'm so glad I did! What I just saw was better than any bestseller," she replies, shooting me a wink.

My insides contract, pulling away from my skin and wrapping into a ball. I just want to curl up and die.

It's one thing to feel superior to Samantha, it's another to have her legitimately hold something over me.

"Sam, wait. You're not going to—" I begin but she cuts me off.

"Are you kidding? Of course I am! The whole town will know your little game. And they don't like being played for suckers, let me tell you." She turns her scowl on Mark, each word dripping with venom. "We may be a small town, but we aren't dumb hicks. Nobody's going to appreciate the two of you making them feel that way."

Annette has appeared next to her at the door and puts a hand on Samantha's shoulder. "I don't appreciate you coming in here without permission, young lady. I think it's time for you to go."

"Can I leave, Annette?" The request bursts out of me, unbidden. All eyes turn to me, and I cringe. "For the rest of the day? Please?" I just can't be here right now. I can't bear Samantha's blistering glee, and I can't even force my eyes in Mark's direction. I just want my bed, a dark room, and maybe enough tequila to knock me out for a few hours.

Annette sighs, and for a second I think she's going to push back.

"Okay." She nods. "If you need to, but please, be back bright and early tomorrow." I'm off my stool before she's even finished her sentence, mumbling my thanks as I push past Samantha. It's all I can do not to look at her. I can feel those hateful eyes drag across me, her smile frozen in place.

"Okay, missy," Annette says to Samantha, her voice edged in ice. "Unless you're going to buy something, I think you're done for the day."

"Of course," Samantha purrs in reply. "I was just leaving. Not much of a reader, anyway."

"I can tell," Annette mutters, just loud enough to be heard.

My bag on my shoulder, I reach out to grab the door handle to leave the shop. But something stops me, and I turn back. Just for a second.

Annette stands at the cash register watching Samantha mosey her way towards the door. I know I only have a second or two before she catches up to me and I can't bear to be near her right now. Even so, I linger just one second more.

To see Mark.

He stands in the doorway to the break room.

And my heart breaks.

His face is so lost. Completely adrift.

What have I done to this man?

sixteen

. . .

Mark

"**E**arth to Mark. Hello? Hey! Snap out of it!"
Blinking furiously, I am shocked back to the present by Annette's sharp tone.

"Sorry," I mumble, readjusting the grip on the screwdriver in my hand. Looking at it, I'm half puzzled as to how it got there. I must have picked it up, but I don't remember. My whole body has been numb since Emily left.

"Mark." Annette snaps her fingers in front of my face. "Focus. Please. For our safety and for the safety of anyone who walks anywhere near this thing." Her voice is slightly less harsh, but only slightly.

"Right." I sigh. I have to get my head in the game.

We're putting the final adjustments on our Spring Festival display and Annette isn't as capable of a set of hands as Emily. But she'll have to do because Emily has called out sick for the second day in a row.

She told Annette it was a cold, but we both know what's really going on. Frankly, the first day was pretty much expected. But when she called this morning, it was more alarming. At least to me. I have no idea how our boss feels about it. Annette and I have not exchanged a word on the subject.

Which is probably for the best because I'm not sure what exactly I'd have to say.

"Okay." Annette redirects my scattered energy back to the task at hand. "Now, I'll hold this piece in place, and you screw it in."

"Sure, sure," I say, shaking my head to clear Emily from my thoughts. It's a lost cause. Emily is never *not* on my mind. But if she's choosing to avoid her job—and me—there isn't much I can do about it. At least I've had the sense to leave her alone.

Which has been a herculean feat.

And I don't know how much longer I can do it.

A sudden jab of pain shoots up my arm, and I yelp as I look down and see a small puncture mark in my hand. Did I really just manage to stab myself with the screwdriver?

"Watch it, Mark!" Annette rebukes sharply. She puts down the piece of the sign she's holding and grabs my hand, inspecting the wound. As she does, her face and voice soften, and those gray-green eyes look into mine. She may be a tough customer on the outside, but her heart is made of pure gold.

"Hey. This is serious, huh? This thing with Emily?"

"Is it that obvious?" I ask feebly.

"As transparent as Saran wrap," she replies. "Trouble is, I don't know how long it's been going on, or how bad you have it." Examining my hand again, she winces lightly. "Let's get you a band-aid and you're going to tell me all about it."

We pack up the few tools we have, and Annette fishes the first-aid kit out from under the cash register to get a bandage.

"Sit," she instructs, pushing me onto the stool. The same one Emily sat on two days ago.

Will she ever not be in my head?

I do as I'm told, only too willing to let my boss push me around.

"Talk," she barks, peeling back the wrapper. I take a deep breath, trying to organize my thoughts. It's a lost cause, so I just open my mouth and let the words tumble out in a rush.

"I think I've been in love with Emily from the moment I first saw her. And when her bully ex-boyfriend came along, I agreed to pretend to be her boyfriend. To keep Leon as far away as possible. I know I shouldn't have, but she was so scared, and I just…" Saying it out loud only makes me feel like more of a dope. But I close my eyes and push on. "Anyway, it turned into something else. Something neither one of us expected, and now it's got me acting all goofy and stupid and doing the dumbest things. And now I'm afraid I've bungled everything and lost her. What do I even do?"

It's a rhetorical question in the end because I don't think there is any real answer to be found. Everything feels so lost and desperate.

Annette has finished bandaging my hand and I let my face fall into my palms. I can't look at anything right now, least of all the judging eyes of my boss.

Trouble is, Annette is nothing if not persistent. She pulls my hands away and forces me to meet her gaze.

"Mark. Look at me. Sounds like you got it bad. And I don't blame you. Emily is as good as they get. I know. I've seen a few things in my time. And I'm happy for you."

""Happy?" I snort. "How does that work?"

"It doesn't seem like it right now. And if you keep this up, you don't stand a chance."

I collapse into myself, ashamed for letting myself be such a mess.

"But," Annette continues. "What Emily needs right now isn't a lover or a boyfriend. She needs a *friend*. Without expectations of any kind. Be that. Prove that you can be that and maybe, just *maybe*, she'll see you in the same light that you see her. But keep pushing and you'll wind up losing her entirely."

The self-pity crowding in my chest dissolves, replaced by something else. Something like resolution, maybe? I'm not sure. But it feels a little better than the weight I've been carrying around everywhere.

Because of course Annette is right.

"Thanks, Annette. I needed to hear that."

She actually allows herself to smile. It's more of a terse horizontal line underneath her nose, but coming from Annette it's close enough.

"Atta boy. Now, why don't you take a little break and get some fresh air? Let me close up."

I nod, grateful for her kindness. My hand is throbbing, and I could use some time away from the shop. It's like Emily's ghost is hanging out around the end of every shelf, which isn't exactly helping.

"Thanks," I say, sliding off the stool.

Annette nods and replies, "Don't mention it. And be careful going home, you're already banged up enough as it is."

I chuckle, leaving the break room and heading for the door.

Just before I turn the handle a book title captures my eye. A slim volume with a cheery lime-green cover. It's a book that's been making waves on the poetry circuit, and we just got a copy in stock.

Normally I'm not much of a poetry person, but for some reason it calls out to me. Flipping it over, my mouth falls open. It's a collection of poems on the power of friendship. In all its forms. Friendship with children, with older people, with animals. And between adults.

It's perfect.

"I'm just gonna buy this…" I call out to Annette, slipping the money into the register before heading out. It feels so serendipitous I don't even take my employee discount. Why tempt fate?

My steps feel a little lighter as I walk to my car. I'm not perfect by any means but I feel I have a little bit more footing in an otherwise topsy-turvy world.

In my car, I find the pen I always keep in my glovebox and scribble a note. Nothing fancy. Nothing over the top. Just a few words:

Emily,

I know I messed up. But you are my friend, first and foremost. I hope you feel the same.

Mark.

Within minutes, I'm outside her apartment and before I can lose my nerve, I slide it through the mail slot.

"Here goes nothing," I mumble to the clanging metal flap. Tempting as it is to linger at her door, I force myself into my car and drive away.

Whatever happens now, it's out of my hands.

seventeen

. . . .

Emily

Brenda and Gertie huddle together next to the potatoes and onions, whispering like they want the whole world to hear them.

"Think she'll make a decision soon?" Brenda asks. Even knowing they've been watching me, it takes me a second to register the 'she' they are referring to is me. My hand hovers in mid-air, somewhere between the bananas and the navel oranges.

"Not sure. Evidently, she's not the best when it comes to picking things."

"You can say that again!"

Both women cackle with their hands over their mouths before pushing their carts towards the bread section. They think they're being sneaky, but they're loud enough to be heard across the entire produce section.

I grab the nearest bunch of bananas and shuffle into the safety of the deli department.

I'm being mocked for picking groceries now?

God, this is so much worse than I could ever have expected. Can I blame them, though? My tiny scandal has to be the most exciting thing to happen in Cider Mill Valley for a while.

The whole town knows about my fake relationship with Mark, and they are doing a poor job of pretending like they don't.

Just about as poor a job as I'm doing sorting out my actual feelings for Mark.

It all feels so overwhelming I wind up abandoning the rest of my grocery shopping, cutting my basket adrift somewhere in the cheese aisle. As I leave the store, I feel a twinge of guilt for the poor stock boy that will have to return the few items I picked up, but I can't stomach staying in there any longer.

I have to get a hold of myself. My life is one great big mess.

"You okay?" Dillard calls from the registers as I fly past. "You haven't finished your—"

"Gotta go," I say, whisking out into the parking lot as fast as I can.

Slumping behind the steering wheel, my gaze drifts to the glaring patch of green poking out from a pile of bags in the passenger seat. I'm not the neatest when it comes to my car. Even half buried, that little book glows like it's radioactive.

The little gift Mark put through my mail slot feels like a rebuke. A needling reminder of how many ways I've screwed up these past few weeks.

Taking the book in both hands, I stare at it, then flip open the cover to read Mark's note for the ten thousandth time. I've memorized it by now. Not that it was difficult. Twenty one little words all lined up in his scrolling, looping handwriting. Looking at it is irresistible to me. Even if it hurts. Which it most certainly does.

"I don't want to," I say out loud to the book. "I don't want to have these feelings. I just want to make a clean break."

And there it is.

A slice of calm, blistering clarity creeps into my bruised heart.

Mark's message about friendship, and this odd book of poetry only makes it all more confusing. The fact that some of the poems tip dangerously close to love letters mixes messages until I'm seeing double.

Top that with all the swirling feelings I have about him—and the embarrassment of how public everything is—makes my next moves very clear.

Jamming my key into the ignition, I set my jaw and start to drive. A deep sense of resolve steals over me. The kind of deadly calm that can only come when ugly decisions get made.

"Emily," Annette says, her eyebrow arched. "What are you saying?"

"I wish I could give you two weeks' notice," I reply, my voice almost robotic. "But I'm afraid I just can't. Brittany told me I could join her anytime, and I feel like speed is of the essence. I'm finally making my move to the big city. She says there are margarita stations there. I'm gonna have a great time!"

The smile on my face is taut like it's made of plastic. Hell, even I'm not convinced. I sound like a badly recorded radio commercial, but I can't stay here. I just can't.

I'm gonna take Brittany up on her offer—even if she doesn't know it yet. Most importantly, I'm getting out of Cider Mill Valley once and for all. It's been a long time coming and now I finally have a good reason.

Annette says nothing for a second, instead cocking her hand on her hip and looking at me from the corner of her eye.

"You got a job lined up in the big, bad city?" she finally asks. "It's expensive there, you know."

"I know." I shrug. "No job yet, but I'll figure something out. I have savings. I can sell my car if it comes to that. Can I use you as a reference on job applications? I know not giving you a full two weeks isn't the best, but…"

I'm rambling now, talking at top speed, like a tape recorder on fast-forward.

Annette doesn't move a muscle.

"And your friend is cool with you moving in with her?"

"Yup. Yup she is," I insist, though I really have no idea. It's been weeks since I last spoke with her. What if she doesn't want me to move there anymore? Are we even still friends? She might be sore that I haven't reached out. Not that I'd blame her if she was. I'd just add her to the list of people I've let down.

"And what about Mark?" Annette asks. Just hearing his name is like a punch to my solar plexus. I try not to let it show but probably do a poor job of it.

"What about him?" My attempt to sound blasé fails miserably.

"You might want to talk to him. At least air things out before you go."

"I… I can't," I say, my voice little more than a squeak as my throat clenches around my sadness. Tears threaten at the edges of my vision. "It hurts too much."

Before I can say another word, Annette sweeps me into a hug. She isn't much of a hugger, but when she gives one it's pretty legendary. I allow myself to be taken in, supported by her. It feels good to lean on someone. Literally and figuratively.

For a long time, we stand with her arms wrapped around me, my tears soaking her shoulder. I finally pull away when the embarrassment of seeing the blooming wet mark on her shirt becomes too much.

"Sorry," I mumble, wiping my nose on my wrist. She just waves me off.

"I've had worse," she says, a smile tugging at the corner of her mouth.

"Thank you. For that," I say, a sense of true release washing over me. At least I got *some* of my sadness out. It still creeps around the edges of my thoughts but at least I can function a little.

Until it comes back, that is.

"I want to offer a counterproposal," Annette says, both her hands resting on my shoulders. She looks at me dead in the eye.

"What's that?" I ask, apprehension slipping in between my ribs.

"Stay until after the Spring Festival." My first reaction is to say no, but Annette sees this and grips my shoulders harder. "I need the hands. And the help. You'd be doing me a huge favor and not leaving me in the lurch in the process. If you still want to leave after that, I'll help you pack. Hell, I'll even drive some of your stuff to the big city and get you settled. But if you'd stay until then, it would help me a ton. Do you think you can do that?"

Guilt prickles at me. How could I leave her hanging on the cusp of the biggest day of the year for her business? She's right, of course and I can't reward her kindness with a refusal.

I consent with a small nod, and she rubs my upper arms.

"Thank you. You'd better be ready for the best reference of your life. Employers will be fighting over you. Now, I'm gonna get back out to the front. God knows those books don't sell themselves." With that, she leaves me alone in the back room. It's my first time back here since Samantha barged in on us, and the room has an eerie quality to it. Like I expect Mark to walk in at any moment, that bereft, hangdog look on his face. Thankfully he has the day off.

I loiter for a few minutes thinking about him before

joining her out in front. I feel a little lighter, but I'll admit I'm still anxious about the coming days with Mark. Being in Cider Mill Valley a little bit longer, I'm bound to run into him. Heck, we're going to work the Spring Festival side by side. I wonder what I'm going to say?

Shaking my head to dispel the thought, I try to focus on the practicals. I need to pack. I need to talk to Brittany. There is still so much to do.

Busying myself with some paperbacks in the non-fiction section, I mull over Annette's words.

Then, with a start, I realize something. She said the word *if*.

"If you still want to leave…"

For me, it's not a question of *if*. It's a question of *when*.

I exhale sharply through my nose and get back to work.

eighteen

. . .

Mark

"I'm gonna get some lemonade. Need anything?" Annette asks as I grunt and sweat my way into finishing up the Spring Festival display.

Stepping back, I wipe my brow, inspecting my work.

"Nah, I'm good for right now," I say, at least a little proud of my handiwork. "Thank you, though."

"Suit yourself." She turns and heads off down the street for the tiny corner store. Bracing my hands on my hips, I ease back further to take it all in. The sign looks good. Better than I would have imagined, even. The looping script and the welcoming paint colors—all Annette's contributions—are ably held up by my carpentry skills. It's eye-catching for sure. No question it'll bring in customers.

At least, I hope so. I need a win now more than ever. Even a little one.

"Hold on," I mutter to myself, seeing a sharp edge that could potentially snag a passerby. "That's annoying." I kneel down to rifle through my toolbox for some sandpaper. As I bend over, I hear two voices I'd much rather avoid.

The sound makes me freeze—halfway between a bend and a squat.

"It's true then?" Leon's gravelly voice cuts through the morning. "I'll be a son of a bitch. Emily is really leaving Cider Mill Valley for good?" My hands instantly stop moving, trapped inside the toolbox.

"Yup." Samantha crows. "As soon as she can. Little Miss Perfect can't take the heat, I suppose." Her voice arches and twists in a sing-song tone that grates my very last nerve. I stand upright, blowing my cover. Not that I give a damn. I want them to know I'm there.

They both stop talking immediately, but if there's any surprise, they hide it well. Samantha wears a fluffy dress that looks almost comical, flashing a wry smile my way. Leon— wearing his customary black like a poor man's Lone Ranger —gives me a dead-eyed stare.

For several long moments, no one speaks. I'm sure as hell not making the first move.

In the end, it's Leon who breaks the silence.

"How about that, Fake Romeo? Your so-called girlfriend pulling up stakes and getting out. Guess you didn't play your part well enough."

I search his face, trying to detect the lie. Unfortunately for me, I come up empty.

"Not true," I say, doing my level best to believe my own conviction. It's a losing battle.

Samantha makes a sad *tsk-tsk* sound, nodding her head slowly, her blue eyes looking at me with mock pity.

"'Fraid so, bub. Your relationship may have been fake, but she's making this move for real."

My heart shatters into tiny pieces in my chest. If there were a strong wind, it'd blow all those pieces away. My throat goes dry, and I blink rapidly to keep back the sting of tears that threaten.

Don't cry in front of these monsters. Don't.

I force myself to stay rigidly calm—at least on the outside.

Leon looks at me, his expression cold and inscrutable.

"Why should you even care?" A nasty smile cuts across his face. "It's not like anything was real. Just some big, stupid game to make me—what? Jealous? Of what, exactly? *You?*"

Leon chuckles at his own taunt and Samantha joins him, her high, tinkling laugh like nails on a chalkboard.

"You never deserved her," I say, my voice low and cold.

That's all I can think of to say. If I let anything else out, I don't think I'd be able to stop. It would either end up with me in tears on the ground or in jail for punching Leon's lights out.

Both are out of the question.

Leon drapes an arm over Samantha's pointy shoulders, pulling her close. I can tell she enjoys the attention, leaning into his body, her face hopeful.

Jesus, they are perfect for each other.

"What does it even matter?" he asks. "Once she's in the city, she'll be surrounded by men way worse than me. Trust me, she'll come crawling back inside of a month. I might even be able to swing back through and pick up with her where we left off." Leon laughs heartily at his own sick fantasy, but Samantha doesn't join in. She clearly hates this turn of events, and instead of pity, I feel the smallest spark of retribution. Her laughter has died away and she looks at Leon with pain and jealousy on her face.

Leon—as usual—appears oblivious.

I seize the chance.

"Seems to me you have the perfect match right next to you. You two are great for each other. Two shallow losers side by side. What more could you want?"

My wisecrack hits Samantha like an arrow. She winces as

if she's been slapped and shrinks away. Leon merely bats my comment away, shifting his weight onto his other foot, his dark eyes scanning the street. He's already bored.

"Nah. The girls of Cider Mill Valley aren't quite my type. I'm starting to see that now. These small-town girls are kinda disposable, you know? Fun for a while but then I have to get back to the big city where the real women are."

He shoots me a look, his expression changing from smug to conspiratorial.

"Maybe you should stand to learn that lesson, bro."

A bonfire of rage ignites within me, and my hands itch for the screwdriver and hammer in my toolbox. It's all I can do not to grab them both and smash them into his face.

Keep your temper in check.

I take a deep breath.

That's when I hear the gasp. Samantha has pulled away from Leon, her face filled with hurt. It's hitting her all at once. She's been nothing but a pawn in this bastard's game this whole time. He's been playing tricks of his own, and she's just now seeing it. Except unlike me, she never agreed to play a part. He just used her.

And now she's learning just how worthless she is in his eyes.

"Keep moving, Leon," I say, my anger coalescing into something else. Something far more useful. "I have work to do."

"I was just leaving anyway. Have to head to a meeting. An *important* one," he snarls, moving down the sidewalk.

"Sure, sure." True or not, I won't give him the satisfaction of thinking it matters to me in the slightest.

"I..." Samantha begins, her voice tiny. I turn back to face her, and she looks so small. Like a wounded bird flapping its wings but unable to fly.

"You're not disposable," I say, surprising us both with my kindness. "No one is."

Tears pool in her eyes.

"How do you know?"

I see now what I have to do. What has been staring me in the face all along. And if I don't do it soon, I'll regret it forever.

"I just do," I reply.

nineteen

. . .

Emily

"You want some lemonade?" Annette calls out. "Smithers has a stand a block down. You know they have the *good* stuff." Tucking some float money into her fanny pack and adjusting her sun visor, she trots along, wholly in her element. Part of me—the part that still can feel happiness—smiles inside. Annette is a demon for lemonade.

"I'm okay, thanks." I give her a wan smile and survey the growing crowd on the street.

"If you say so. I'll be right back. Hold down the fort." She disappears into the throng of people.

I think it's the most highly attended Spring Festival I've ever seen. And I've seen them all. But the winter was long, and people are eager to be out again, even if the weather is still a bit on the chilly side. Everyone ignores it, embracing the idea of summer. Even the light jackets and jeans can't dampen the collective spirits. Lemonade, hot dogs, cotton candy. The works.

I just wish I could work myself up to enjoy it as much as everyone else seems to.

The aromas of the food area waft down towards our little set-up right outside the store. We've put up a tent, a few folding tables, along with *lots* of books. And of course, the huge sign that Mark and I designed. Even if I did leave the actual building of it up to him and Annette.

I feel exposed being out here alone. Which is a little foolish because I'm in the middle of a moving sea of people. Folks amble by, their eyes casting glances over the books; some smiling, some not.

As if every single person knows me to be a fraudster. The kind of sad person who has to *invent* a romantic life. Phonier than anything between the pages stacked up around me.

Don't be dramatic, Emily. There are lots of people here who don't even know you.

It's true. The Festival is popular and people from areas all around Cider Mill Valley make the drive over, but I can't help feeling that the locals have let them in on the secret. As if some giant memo went out that I never saw: watch out for Emily at the book booth. She's a pathetic loser. And a liar.

"You all alone?" an older man asks, the question nagging at me as he thumbs through the latest crime thriller.

Why am I alone? Where's Mark? Why is it just Annette and I manning the booth?

I mean, she made me delay my departure to the big city because of this. Surely, he should help out too? So, where is he?

"Uhhh, not quite," I reply, forcing a smile. "Some of my co-workers are here. The owner's just getting lemonade."

The man nods approvingly. "Believe me, I understand that. Best lemonade in a 50-mile radius." He turns the book over in his hands. It's got an identical cover to all the other crime thrillers that seem to sell better than anything else in the store. Why should that one in particular catch his eye?

"Where's that tall handsome fella who works with you?" The description catches me in the throat.

"Mark?"

"That's his name—Mark." He snaps his fingers as if the name was just on the tip of his tongue the whole time. "Such a nice young man. I'm sure you agree?" There's a knowing glimmer in his eye that puts me even more off center.

"Yes," I stammer. "Yes, he is. Very nice."

"Well. Just know that a lot of us around here are rooting for you two."

Did he really just say that?

I open my mouth to reply but can't seem to find any words. Are people really talking about us like that? Do they actually *want* our relationship to be real?

"Anyway." The older man takes another look at the book, then lays it back on a stack. "I'm gonna wait till that's in paperback. These hardcovers are too rich for this retiree. You have yourself a good day."

"You too," I mumble, straightening the book on the pile. My fingers are numb, and the whole world kaleidoscopes around me. I've spent so much time hiding from prying eyes out here in the open, it never dawned on me that some might not be as malicious as I thought.

Is it possible some could actually be sympathetic? I don't have time to ponder it.

"Good people of Cider Mill Valley! Can you believe we're already back here at our fabulous Spring Festival?" The PA speakers peppering the main street crackle with the substandard sound system of every small town in America. Everyone hovers where they are, idly listening as they continue to look at the booths, order food, sip drinks.

From my little roost, I've got a dead view of the little stage in the town square. Much as I try not to look, I can't help myself.

Mayor McKean is a rotund, red-faced man who somehow

seems surprised he's the mayor of Cider Mill Valley. But he is and has been for the past three terms. He's the perfect fit for this sleepy town.

"As your mayor, it's one of the highlights of our yearly calendar, and I want to extend a particular thank you to Evergreen Savings Bank for being our chief sponsor this year. Let's give them a generous round of applause!"

McKean leads the crowd in a smattered clap, his face shining already.

Despite there not really being anything to do, I task myself with tidying the booth. Anything to keep my hands busy. I'm all anxious and fidgety, praying the minutes tick by smoothly until the festival ends and we can clean everything up again. Then I can scurry back to my apartment to finish packing.

"As you may know," Mayor McKean continues. "Evergreen has not only been a huge part of this festival, they are unveiling plans for a new Little League stadium, along with some other measures in the town that will really put Cider Mill Valley on the map. In fact, they've overhauled their entire system so if you want to bank in the 21st century, I suggest you hustle on over and open yourself an account!"

I cringe inwardly. Why does he insist on this homey talk? Of course, the locals eat it up. Small town charm, I guess.

"So, I want to introduce you to someone who's been instrumental in all these changes. You may have seen him about town—there aren't too many folks like him here in Cider Mill Valley!" The mayor says nervously, which draws my eyes up again.

Sure enough, I see what he means. Standing right next to him in a dark suit and no tie, looking like a wolf that's wandered into a sheep party, is Leon. He's wearing a smile like he's licking his chops, and smooths his hand over that preposterous slick of hair.

"Leon Carruthers has been the leader on Team Evergreen, getting these initiatives in place. He's one of our own, and I have to say it's a real pleasure to see someone who grew up here come back to help put us on the map. Leon, why don't you tell us what's going on and what the good people of Cider Mill Valley can expect in the coming weeks and months?"

"Thank you, Mayor," Leon croons, his charming smile hovering on the edge of condescension. "Cider Mill Valley is about to join the big cities! We have made changes at Evergreen that will finally lift this town to the place it deserves. Make an appointment with one of our bankers and you'll see what we mean."

He's met with a mixed response. Some are appreciative, others not so much. Cider Mill Valley is a place where people generally like being what they are. They don't want to be like the big cities. For a reason.

Something in me shrinks. What did I ever see in the guy? He's so smug. So sure of himself and not in a good way. His dislike for this town and for all towns like it seems so obvious now. An attitude I once thought was cosmopolitan is now something else entirely. Just downright nasty.

I stare down at my hands, about as miserable as I've ever been. Maybe running away to the city isn't such a great idea after all. But where else can I start over? Have a clean slate?

A screech of feedback over the speakers breaks me out of my solo pity party.

"That's all well and good, *Leon*, but I think the people of Cider Mill Valley like things just the way they are," a new voice says. This one is as warm and welcoming as Leon's is cold and snide.

My eyebrows shoot up.

It's Mark.

Standing there in light blue dress pants and a cream shirt. He looks like everything Leon isn't. Confident without being cocky. Relaxed and sure. The perfect antidote to Leon's condescending smarminess.

He's taken the microphone out of a momentarily stunned Leon's hands. The mayor and one of his assistants stand awkwardly to the side, unsure of just what to do.

"Thanks… uh… Leon," Mark says, snapping his fingers and giving an exaggerated shrug to the audience in a mock apology for seeming to forget Leon's name. He's rewarded with scattered but hearty laughter. "I'm sure that, while the people of Cider Mill Valley appreciate all the *favors* you've done us," *air quotes!* "we're a pretty happy bunch just the way we are!" Mark beams and earns a louder round of applause than Leon could ever hope to muster.

And Leon knows it. His eyes grow dark with anger, but there's not a damn thing he can do about it. For his part, Mayor McKean shrugs cheerfully, seemingly eager as everyone else to see what will happen next. After all, he's in the business of keeping the people of Cider Mill Valley happy, isn't he?

"What you all have here is pretty special," Mark goes on, slipping easily into a bashful familiarity. "I'm fairly new to this town, but I felt it right away. There's a particular way of living here in Cider Mill Valley that appeals to me. It's pretty, it's safe, and it has the best people around."

I could be wrong, but I think his eyes flick my way.

His words draw even more applause, and my heart beats faster in my chest.

What's he doing up there? Somehow, I can't shake the feeling all this is going to end badly. I don't think I can take any more shame or heartache. But something in me quivers at seeing Mark up there, at his boldness.

"I've heard a few people say that you can only find certain things in the big city," Mark says, giving a pointed look to Leon. "But we know that's simply not true. If you look close enough, you'll see what you need right in front of you. Right here in Cider Mill Valley."

My heart thumps so hard, I think it's going to fly out of

my mouth. I take shallow breaths and try to hang on. Now when Mark's gaze swings past the bookstore, there's no doubt he catches sight of me.

"Let me tell you," he says into the microphone. "I know what I have in Cider Mill Valley. And I'm not about to throw that away. I also know that while some of you may be aware of all the ups and downs in my personal life over the past few weeks, I'm here to publicly tell you that I don't care. That what I feel is real. It's one thing to tell all of you, but there's someone else who needs to hear it more."

I think I'm going to faint.

What is he saying? What is happening?

Everyone knows what he's talking about. My throat goes dry as the pinpricks of dozens of eyes sting my skin.

"Emily Young, can you come up here?" Mark asks, the question zinging out over the speakers.

My first instinct is to flee. Just dash out of the booth and run a thousand miles in the opposite direction. But I don't. Something won't let me. Taking a shuddering breath, I try to listen to my heart.

Go to him. Just go. Now.

Looking around, I take note of all the faces turned my way. To my surprise, I find smiles instead of mockery, people nodding in understanding rather than in disdain.

They are saying it too. Go to him.

Suddenly, Annette is there, a comically large beer stein of lemonade in her hand. She nods most of all, practically pushing me towards the stage.

Approaching on unsteady legs, I notice even the mayor's shiny red face bobs in approval. On the periphery, Leon positively quakes with anger. He won't do anything though. He's too exposed up here. Too many people watching.

Leon is many things, but most of all he's a coward.

As soon as I reach the lip of the stage, he fades into the background along with everyone else. I only have eyes for

Mark. Extending his hand, he pulls me towards him, a warm smile on his face.

"Hello, Emily. Thank you," he whispers, holding the microphone away from his face.

"For what?"

Mark gives me a wink and something inside me melts.

"For saying yes, that's all."

His answer is enigmatic. But it makes me smile.

A second later, the microphone is back, our private moment on pause.

"Emily, I've brought you up here in front of everyone—both the people that have known all your life and those who are seeing you for the first time—to ask you something."

I tremble, trying to tune out the crowd, Leon, the mayor.

"Emily, I've spent my life doing the right thing, being a good person, following the rules. And, for the most part, that has served me well. But sometimes, playing by the rules means you don't say the thing you want to say, you don't act on the impulse you want to act on."

Taking my hand, he gives it a squeeze and looks directly in my eyes. I feel the crowd, the noise, the anxiety of being up here on this makeshift stage in front of the whole town, melt away.

"I realized not too long ago that if I did the right thing when it comes to how I feel about you—if I didn't speak up, or didn't follow my heart, I ran the risk of losing you forever. So, Emily Young, I'm throwing that idea away. For right now at least, I'm abandoning what's right. What's proper. And if you'll allow it in the years to come, I'll do it every day from now on."

I give him a quizzical look. My insides churn with a mix of hope, nerves and something else… something I can't even name.

"Marry me, Emily?" My ears start to ring and my knees buckle. But he keeps my hand in his, those assuring eyes keeping me on my feet. "Marry me, and I'll spend the rest of my life doing right by you. Unless…" he adds with another wink, "you ask me not to."

As he asks me this most momentous of all questions, he sinks to one knee, pulling out a ring from his pocket.

Collective gasps and sighs ring out from the crowd. Some part of me clocks a grunt of disgust from Leon, but none of it matters.

A wellspring of happiness bursts open inside me.

This is what you want. Have wanted all this time. He's right there. Kneeling in front of you.

"Yes." The word tumbles out of me, joyous and fizzy. Mark slides the ring onto my finger, deft and sure.

The crowd gasps again, unbottled happiness exploding into a jubilant round of applause. Mark scoops me into a massive hug, whirling me round and round. As we spin and the colors of the world blur and fade, I whisper in his ear.

"But wasn't everything fake?"

He sets me down and takes my face in his hands. The sound of the crowd is deafening, a sweet soundtrack to this most perfect of moments.

"Not to me. It never was."

The kiss he gives me is the stuff of legends.

One thing is for sure.

This year's Spring Festival will be one to remember.

twenty

. . .

Mark

"I'm running out to see my favorite gal," I call to Brenda, who sits at the desk outside of my office. "I'll be back for that trustee meeting at three."

"I thought I was your favorite gal!" she responds, a mock pout in her voice.

"Right! Sorry. Always get you and Emily mixed up!" I toss over my shoulder as I leave the bank, Brenda's chirpy laughter trailing after me.

The sun is on the right side of warm, and there is only a slight spring breeze. I take a big gulp of air. Hard to believe winter is finally over. More amazing still is the fact that it's been a year since the Spring Festival.

Or as I like to call it: The Day Everything Changed For The Better.

That has a nice ring to it.

I whistle as I stop by the local deli, ordering a couple of sandwiches and some chips. Adding a six-pack of my favorite beer to the order at the last second.

"What are you celebrating?" Doug, the deli owner, asks as he rings me up.

"Me? Does it look like I'm celebrating something?"

Doug laughs, handing me my change with a twinkle in his eye.

"Actually, you're right. You look as cheerful today as ever. Guess you're always celebrating something."

I smile, thinking of what I have now—a great job at Evergreen Bank, a bit of money in savings, and best of all— the woman of my dreams.

"You know what," I ask, almost dancing to the door. "You're right. I am."

What a difference a year makes…

Who could have predicted that my bold show of gate-crashing Leon's big speech at last year's Spring Festival would yield me so many rewards?

Evergreen Bank—the big sponsor—took notice of it for sure. After the hubbub of the day died down, they reached out requesting a job interview for their new bank manager position. Said they liked my 'pluck' and my 'zeal.'

Said I'd be the perfect fit.

After a year of hard work, I've got a portfolio of satisfied customers, a secretary that makes the best damn coffee in the state, and the freedom to make the bank better for our customers. If the guys over at corporate think I'm a perfect fit, I would have to agree that they're right.

Still whistling, I see the facade of the bookstore come into view and I smile even more.

I must look like a fool, I say to myself, then I realize I don't care.

"If people think that, that's on them," I whisper to myself.

The bell above the door announces my arrival, and I top it by calling out, "Hello there!"

Annette is at the register pretending to frown, but the gal I came to see is up on a step ladder off to the side with a wide grin on her face.

"Whoa! That's a lot of real estate you got there," I observe, my eyes trailing over the display that Emily is working on.

The last twelve months have seen a lot of changes for Emily too. Positive ones.

Her art has become so popular in town she's had to expand. Cards sell almost before the ink is dry. Annette never misses a solid business opportunity if she can help it, so she's allowed Emily's work to take over more and more of the bookshop.

There's no denying her art brings in customers. Annette gets a percentage of whatever gets sold, and along the way people usually buy some books.

It's a win-win for all involved, and makes Cider Mill Valley that much cooler.

"Make anyone rich today?" Emily quips as she descends the ladder and plants a kiss on me. The smell of her vanilla skin still sends me.

"Oh sure! Rockefellers and Vanderbilts lining up outside," I joke back, setting down the bag with the sandwiches and beers.

"Good!"

"How about you? This is looking great," I exclaim.

"Thanks. It really is," she replies, looking over the assembled canvases, cards, and prints. "I'm so lucky to have an opportunity like this. Gallery percentages are just so crazy." Emily looks over at Annette who gives a wave.

"That's right," Annette crows. "I'm a true patron of the arts!" Her jagged edges have worn down a bit and there are times when she's downright *cuddly*. Nice to see Emily and I aren't the only ones flourishing around here.

I step closer to my beautiful bride, holding her close. Her proximity still makes me dizzy, my body still keenly reacts to her every curve.

"I'm so proud of you, baby," I whisper.

Emily giggles, wiggling out of my grip.

"Hey! You two!" Annette hollers across the store, her eyes sparkling. "This is a family-friendly organization! Take it in the back room!"

"You sure?" Emily asks with a wicked glint in her eye.

"What do you mean? Am I sure? Course I am! Not every day Mr. Fancy Bank Manager comes by!" Which is about as big a lie as there is—I'm here virtually every afternoon.

"You heard her," I mutter as Emily takes me by the hand and leads me to the familiar break room—the site of so many of our formative moments together.

"Thanks, Annette," I quip over my shoulder.

"Anytime," she replies. "Besides, I want to talk about that line of credit soon."

"Course! Just come on by the bank. We'll get you all set up." With that the door closes and it's just me and Emily. The coziness of the room hugs in around us, the smell of paper and dust familiar and comforting.

"What'd you bring?" Emily asks, perching on a stool. "I'm famished."

"Good. I have a meatball or turkey club," I say, pulling out both sandwiches and a small mountain of napkins. "Take your pick."

Emily thinks for a second, absently rubbing her stomach.

"Mmmm… split them?" she asks.

"Capital idea." Taking a plastic knife from among the art supplies, I halve the sandwiches, and we settle in. She must have been hungry because we fall silent as soon as we start eating. Not that I mind. Being with Emily always brings me pleasure whether we're talking or not.

"Oh, I almost forgot," I say, breaking the silence. "I brought a little something-something to wash these down with. But don't tell anyone, least of all your boss." I hunch over, looking conspiratorial and silly all at once as I slide one of the beers from my bag.

Emily laughs—a little too loudly.

"Shh! Are you trying to blow our cover? I know we aren't supposed to drink while we're on the clock but maybe we can split one?" I arch my eyebrows and Emily laughs again—even louder this time.

"Em! What are you doing?" I reply, dropping my act. Though I'm sure Annette wouldn't mind, I'd rather not have that conversation.

"Oh, Mark! That's sweet of you. And believe me, I'd *love* to share one with you, but I can't." She's smiling even as she says no. A weird set of mixed messages. Cute on her, to be sure, but confusing all the same.

"But I don't understand. You love a good beer. We have them all the time."

Emily laughs again.

"I know we do. But I have to take a break from them for a while."

She flashes me a mischievous grin. Somewhere in the back of my brain, something flares up. Excitement, maybe?

"But why?"

Emily doesn't answer me with words. She kisses me. Long and warm and loving. I melt a little and relax into it. No one kisses like the woman I love.

After a blissful moment Emily pulls back, looking me deep in the eyes.

"I can't drink beer right now because of this," she says, taking my hand and placing it on her stomach. I could pass out I'm so overcome.

"I... what? Really?" I can barely form words, let alone an articulate question. Thankfully Emily saves me the trouble.

"Yes, really."

I take her in my arms, joy radiating all around us. She squeezes me back, cheeks wet with happy tears.

Just when I thought my year couldn't get any better, it has. I ask myself the same question I do a thousand times every single day. Every time I think about Emily and the life we've built together.

How did I get so lucky?

epilogue

. . .

Emily

"Is it going to fit?" I ask nervously as we wait in the vestibule of the real estate office. "Did you measure the front door?" Mark doesn't answer right away, but he takes my hand in his, gives it a squeeze and lifts it to his lips to kiss my fingers.

"Your yellow couch? It'll fit. We'll figure it out. I promise." He smiles, almost laughing. God, I wish I could tap into his ease. Just a dash of his confidence would settle me right down. But nope. True to form, I'm an absolute bundle of nerves.

"Are you sure?"

Mark looks at me from the corner of his eye, bemused.

"Is that all you're worried about? Whether we can get your couch into the house?"

I sigh, trying to ease the tension in my shoulders. It's a losing battle. Looking down, I marvel once again at the growing bump where my flat stomach used to be. I can't see my feet, though I can certainly feel them. They have been slightly swollen since the day I hit the halfway mark.

Can't complain, though. This pregnancy has been a dream.

It really has. No sickness, barely any weird cravings. Just enjoying the marvelous changes to my body as this baby—our baby—grows inside me.

But then a lilting voice calls out through an open door, "Are you two ready?" and I'm all sixes and sevens again. It's Wendy, our real estate agent. She and the seller's agent are just on the other side of a conference room window, shuffling and re-shuffling a seemingly endless mountain of paper with the bank representative.

As they neaten them into a stack the reality of it blossoms over me. These papers are about to be covered in my signature, and Mark's.

If all goes well, that is.

"Ready as I'll ever be," Mark replies. How can he be so confident? So chipper? I'm sweating bullets over here!

He gets to his feet, still holding my hand. I stop him by squeezing his fingers.

"What if it all falls through?" I whisper. "What if the whole deal just collapses?"

"Babe. It'll be fine. I checked the financing myself. Every box and every line. We are good. The house will be ours in a matter of minutes." His voice is warm like a summer's breeze, blowing away the top edge of my anxiety.

"It will?" I ask, sounding more like a frightened child than a grown woman with a baby on the way. My pregnancy has been textbook, but my emotions are something else entirely.

"Yup. And as a bonus—I'll rub your feet after I carry you over the threshold," he says. "How's that for a bargain?"

"Okay." He knows how to win me over every time.

"Great. Now come on, they're waiting."

I let myself be led into the generic-looking conference room where the next thirty minutes fly by in a blur of paper, pens, scribbles and signatures. Finally, the heavy weight of a set of keys landing in the palm of my hand anchors me in place.

"Congratulations! She's all yours!" Wendy croons, her shiny white teeth beaming at me. It's like a bucket of cold water.

We did it. Welcome to the rest of your life.

Why do I feel like we just got away with something?

The house on the edge of Cider Mill Valley is actually ours. Mark and I couldn't believe our luck when it came on the market. It's right at the head of a number of idyllic hiking trails, with adult trees shading the property. When the sellers accepted our offer, I all but passed out. Now that the keys are in my hand, the same woozy, dreamlike feeling blankets over me again.

I don't really pay attention to what happens next. Mark thanks everyone, shakes their hands, all that good stuff. Then his hand warms the small of my back as he escorts me from the office and into the car.

A short drive later we arrive, the tires crunching on the pea gravel. The house practically smiles at us. Red brick and green shutters. Like something out of a picture book.

Maybe I'll write and illustrate one. A delightful story for children about finding the perfect home.

For my perfect family. For a new life that will likely draw on its walls, throw food on its floors, and light up the whole place with laughter.

Mark and I don't get out of the car right away. We sit in contented silence and stare.

"We're home," he says at last.

"Yes. Yes, we are." Just saying it all my anxiety melts away. "And, yeah," I say. "The yellow couch will fit. Easy." Mark bursts into laughter and I join in, filling the car with our joy. Then we carry it inside to fill our new home with it as well.

acknowledgments

I never imagined myself to be a writer. It was something I enjoyed doing, but didn't trust my abilities. Turns out, it takes a global pandemic and the encouragement of my editor to push me into sending the sample that launched me into ghostwriting. Thanks, Dan Hodge, for seeing something I couldn't.

Thanks to all my English teachers who let me wander away from my assignments and just write whatever I wanted. I'll always be grateful for that freedom.

Special thanks to my mother who introduced me to the world of Jane Austen and Charlotte Brontë. While I can't aspire to write like them, I sure enjoy their words today.

Thanks to my husband Damon and my son Julian for giving me the space to write, the encouragement to do so, and an ear when I needed it. And of course, the warmth (and distraction) of my cats, Rosie, Riggles and the irascible Toast. Love you all – always.

about the author

Charlotte Northeast spent time during the pandemic lurking in the shadows of ghostwriting but is now proud to be out in the open. She has written books across several different genres: rom-com, sci-fi, religious and fantasy.

Her career started in the theatre where she is an actor, director and writer. She is one quarter of the writing team of *The Complete Works of Jane Austen, Abridged* (also a performer). Her adaptation of Thomas Heywood's *Fair Maid of the West Parts 1 and 2* was an audience favorite, and a critical success for the Philadelphia Artists' Collective (PAC) in 2015.

Since then, she has adapted Fletcher's *Tamer Tamed*, and been a devising mind behind several shows, including *You Shouldn't Be Doing What You're Doing On That Ladder* and *Citrus Andronicus*.

Charlotte lives in Collingswood, NJ with her husband, son and two ridiculous cats.

www.ingramcontent.com/pod-product-compliance
Lightning Source LLC
Chambersburg PA
CBHW010612310726
48969CB00010B/2668